THROW THE TEXAS DOG A BONE

An Al Quinn Novel

RUSS HALL

Unlocking New Worlds

Throw the Texas Dog a Bone
A Red Adept Publishing Book

Red Adept Publishing, LLC
104 Bugenfield Court
Garner, NC 27529
http://RedAdeptPublishing.com/

First Print Edition: July 2016

Print ISBN-13: 978-1-940215-72-3
Print ISBN-10: 1-940215-72-2

Cover and Formatting: Streetlight Graphics

Every dog has its day!

CHAPTER ONE

THE BARKING AND YELPING ROSE to a crescendo, some dog voices eager and happy, others hysterical, baying, and desperate—all frantic to greet Al Quinn.

He took in the bouncing faces, flopping ears, and wagging tails, even a few lunging growls with snarling jaws pressed to the kennel doors. Finally, the smells swept over and dominated him—not dog droppings, as he'd expected, but an ammonia cloud wafting from the adjacent cat shelter.

A recent round of antiseptic cleaning products sought to overpower the combined odors of what looked to Al like at least forty pure breeds of dogs and as many more creative mixtures derived from seemingly impossible matches. *A dachshund with a stepladder?*

Al wore a pale-blue denim shirt, khaki slacks, and boots, looking no different as a retired sheriff's deputy than he had as an active one. Sheriff Clayton had insisted he still carry the badge.

He recognized only a few of the breeds and had to guess at most of the others as he crossed the parking lot to the shelter entrance. He recalled why he had never visited a public animal shelter before. When pet-adoption societies set up a row of cages outside mall stores, he could barely get past the begging eyes that peered up at him from behind the bars. *"Take me home. Let me love you unconditionally. Please. Please. Please."*

The front entrance of the shelter funneled its visitors through an initial set of holding pens between two large glassed-in displays of photos pinned to corkboards that showed all the recent adopters with their pets. Al paused to look. Probably shouldn't have, but it was a feel-good moment in contrast to all the desperate barking. A mastiff lay stretched out asleep on a couch beside his sleeping human, a bearded man in a checkered flannel shirt. In another photo, a small boy had an arm around the shoulders of a half pointer–half boxer while his mother and father beamed down at them both. Each of the pictures told a story. Some were accompanied by happy letters from new owners. In all, the effect had been carefully orchestrated by someone who knew how to pluck the strings of the human heart like a harp. Al would have done the same himself if his charge was to save and restore the abandoned, abused, and underappreciated living furry remnants of some people's lives. Sell the positives, the benefits.

The shelter lay nestled in a snug canyon of steep rock walls, the sort found in the hill country west of Austin, an area full of sharp ups and downs that surprised visitors who thought Texas was flat. The surrounding hard stone surfaces caught the frantic barking of the dogs, echoing and magnifying the din. Someone had planted saplings around the facility, and a soaker hose was helping them along. A breeze swirled along past the canyon walls to lift and swoop down to rattle the few leaves on the trees. The budget hadn't allowed for planting bigger trees, but someone with vision and a long-term commitment to the site was thinking ahead toward growing an acoustic buffer so the noise would be less harsh. *Thoughtful. Very thoughtful.*

The thing was, the trees were pecans and live oaks, hardy drought-resistant stock that could do well once their taproots were established. They'd be a legacy someday but wouldn't do much good for the next few years. They were too slow to grow. A few hundred years in the future, they would provide shade and insulate the shelter, though Al doubted he or anyone connected with the place would be around. He'd have planted sycamores, an old bank-landscaping trick, since they would've grown quickly and given the business a look of being staid, established, of having been around a long while.

Al stirred himself to move on. The first few wire-mesh cages on either side held what he suspected were the cheeriest of the dogs of those waiting to be adopted. To his right, a dog that looked like a whippet was bouncing around in antic joy, as if it owned four pogo sticks for legs. To his left, a stately female named Coco, an English pointer, pressed a wet nose against the wires of her cage. Next, on Al's right, a small Australian cattle dog mix with bent ears and a tilted head took in Al with careful eyes that didn't seem to expect much. His name was Tanner. Unlike the other dogs, he seemed resigned or, at the least, not pushy with his neediness. He maintained a quite dignified reserve, not hoping for much and getting what he expected.

Al walked on past the other cages. At the front door to the shelter's office, he veered right and went around the building, headed toward the sinister structure at the far end of the lot, a large oven, where he expected to find the ME. Clive Barnes's station wagon, a silver Volvo, was parked close. His assistant, Teddy, was stretching yellow tape around the scene. She had mousy brown hair and looked downward while unrolling the tape from its spool. Her stocky build, along with the frown she often wore, made her look tougher than she was. Al knew she had a

3

secret fascination with movie celebrities and also a heart about as big as the state.

Clive lifted his head from a small pile of bones he was sifting through. He had dressed much the same as Al and had thinning hair turning from gray to white, which he kept buzzed short to keep it out of his way. He rubbed at his forehead and left a streak of soot as he did.

"Are you sure they're human, Clive?" Al asked, lifting a stretch of tape to duck under it.

"Well, the thing is, Al, the reason they send you to medical school is to make sure you can readily make that distinction. What do you know about cremations?"

"I know that skin melts at about two hundred degrees Fahrenheit. But bones, which contain a lot of calcium phosphate, lose their organic mass at about one thousand one hundred twelve degrees or so, which is why crematories for humans generally run at about eighteen hundred degrees. Even then, some bone fragments often remain because their melting point is so high, so the crematoria put the fragments into a grinder that smashes them into powder to be combined with the rest of the ashes—all part of the courtesy so the next of kin can toss Aunt Lizzy into the waves, or whatever she requested, without any unpleasantness."

Clive tilted his head. "How long were you a detective for the sheriff's department before you retired?"

"I was in the department for thirty-two years, at least twenty of those as detective. Why?"

"Did you ever forget anything?"

"Nothing of vital importance." Al glanced back toward where the dogs were still kicking up a fuss.

"You've got a memory that would make an elephant blush." Clive glanced toward the shelter, where the dogs were still barking. "You aren't thinking of adopting, are you? Coming out here can have that effect."

With his post-heart-attack brother, Maury, staying at his lakeside house along with his nurse, Bonnie, as well as Fergie, an old friend he wished was more than an old friend, not to mention a front yard full of deer he had fed all the way through the recent drought, Al had no business even thinking about bringing a dog home. He shook his head. "Furthest thing from my mind."

"Well, I, for one, am glad you came back from retirement to fill in until Clayton hires or appoints someone new."

"So we have human bones. What now?"

Teddy was hanging close, not missing a word. A lot of people in the department thought her a little slow since she had a touch of autism, dyslexia, and who knew what else. But Al had long suspected she craved being an investigator herself and missed very little in her aspiration to be the best she could be at what she did, though little of real importance had been entrusted to her so far by anyone other than Clive.

"Identification," Clive said.

"Maybe try matching with anyone missing. That ball will be in your court."

"The thing is, there's a wrinkle."

"What kind of wrinkle?" Al asked.

"They're not all from the same person."

"How many?"

"Four, five, maybe even six people."

"Yikes." Al resisted the temptation to run a hand across his brow.

"That was my sentiment as well."

The office door of the rescue center was open, so Al tapped

a knuckle on the wooden frame. The woman behind the paper-covered desk looked up at him.

"Come on in," she said. "I'm just trying to stay busy. But I'm too rattled to really get anything done. What's the news from out there?"

"Not good, I'm afraid." Al looked around.

One wall was lined with gray four-drawer file cabinets. A couple of college diplomas and a few pictures hung on the wall behind the desk in the windowless office. Except for the desk, the room was tidy and poised for action in the mission of finding new homes for displaced pets. Two empty guest chairs sat on the near side of the desk. He lowered himself into one of them.

"I'm Myra. Myra Henningdale. This place was my dream. Now, it's turning into my nightmare."

Al took her in, probably a confident woman on most days, in her early forties, with long dark hair that didn't look dyed. Her narrow, handsome face showed lines hinting at frequent smiling and hearty laughter. However, that wasn't her current mood. Her lips trembled as she picked each word with care. Her hazel eyes were worried, but she didn't seem ready to throw in the towel yet. She wore a khaki blouse with big pockets, the kind Al had seen zookeepers wear.

"How many people work here?" Al asked.

"One full time, two part time, and a varying number of volunteers—between fourteen and sixteen, usually." She rubbed a finger along one side of her forehead, seeking and failing to smooth the worry lines.

"You're the full-timer, right?"

"Only if between seventy and ninety hours a week qualifies."

With only 168 hours in a week, Al realized that didn't leave much time for coming and going, home time, and anything else like recreation or a personal life. Al had worked some seventy-to-ninety-hour weeks a few times in his life—hadn't cared for it and didn't recommend it. "That means you're here most of the time."

"There's a fold-up cot in the closet and a small foam mattress. So, not all of that time is at full alert." She tended to pause and chew the inside of her mouth before answering some questions and again after giving the answers, which wasn't unusual, but if the situation at the shelter went the wrong way, the inside of her mouth might need medical attention. "So, you want to know if any of my people, semiregular or volunteer, are missing. No, they're not. Are you sure about...?"

"The ME says yes. One of your workers spotted the bones, right?"

"Yeah. Jeff. He's studying to be a vet. He's off for the semester from A&M. We're lucky to have him. He knows things only a vet can, which is up a notch from raw enthusiasm and compassion. Nothing wrong with those, but there's a lot to do here, and it helps mightily to have someone who actually knows how to do them. We were closing for the day when he spotted the bones. He had me call it in. I know I should have kept him around, but he was pretty jangled. It's a real mess. I can give you a home address, but you may just want to wait until he comes to work tomorrow."

"And?" Al coaxed.

"Megan. She's my gal Friday. Truth be told, she runs most of the business side of things when she's here while I doctor, fix, and tend to the pets."

Al spotted one other bit of art on the sparsely covered left wall, a cartoon, framed behind no-glare glass. A dog was leaning out of a car window, his ears flapping. He was shouting to another dog the car was passing on the street, "Hey, I'm going off to get tutored."

The corner of Al's mouth twitched. He liked that Myra had a sense of humor. That added a dimension to her, one she needed right then, tired and exasperated as she looked. She probably hadn't pictured entertaining a crime-scene crew when she'd made all the sacrifices to embrace the vocation she'd chosen. "Why are you located here? It's a little out of the way," Al said.

"Not too far from the city for people to come look at prospective pets but far enough out the land was affordable. We're on a reasonably busy road, especially for people coming to and from Lake Travis to boat, picnic, or recreate. Plus, these days we can reach people through the Internet. You'd be surprised how many people look for their pets from their home computers."

"Not really." Al glanced at the side wall as if half expecting a window to have grown there since he'd come in. A window would have been a nice touch to the office. "Let me ask you something. You've positioned this shelter as a 'no kill' facility, yet you have a place to cremate remains. Why is that?"

Myra sighed. She looked at a spot somewhere over Al's shoulder, perhaps reading from some mental script. "Back about the time I was born, in the 1970s, American shelters euthanized twelve to twenty million dogs and cats a year, at a time when there were sixty-seven million pets in homes. Nowadays, shelters euthanize around four million animals all told a year while there are more than one hundred thirty-five million dogs and cats in homes. That's a pretty darn big decline in euthanasia numbers— from around twenty-five percent of American dogs and cats euthanized every year to about three percent—and that represents some substantial progress."

Her eyes lowered and fixed on Al's. She stifled a choke, a little burr of emotion. "The fact is, people still make commitments they can't keep, turn dogs and cats loose, let them populate too freely, and we just have too darn many. There are all kinds of shelters, city ones or the private kind like this one. But all shelters, even the no kill ones—that 'no kill' label is a target, not a stone-cold fact—have to euthanize some of their population. Usually, with dogs, it's when they're too aggressive. With cats, it's mostly from illnesses and occasionally temperament. But, truth be told, when we get crowded and adoption is low, it's the older, unadoptable pets who have to make room. If you look at the little descriptions on each cage, you'll see a penciled number on the lower right corner. That's the number of days an animal has left. I don't like it, but it's the only way. Like most shelters, we use an intravenous injection of as much pentobarbital or sodium thiopental as each pet needs, actually just a bit more than each needs. It's a necessary but hardly pleasant part of what we do since we care about every animal here."

"Do you write all those pet descriptions yourself?"

"Most of them. I don't anthropomorphize as much as Megan does, but I try to tell the story behind each pet, its strong and weak points, and whether it needs special attention. We offer post-adoption training from an outside service for those pets that need it."

"I was just seeking to establish why there's an oven," Al said. "What temperature does it run at?"

"You'd have to ask Jeff for the everyday details. I suspect it's around seven or eight hundred degrees, which is hot but maybe not hot enough. We do what we can, but from an administrative standpoint, it's one of our biggest budget line items. We tried burying them for a while but had a few coyote dig-ups, and the land simply couldn't take it for all we would have for it if we started a fill. So we got the oven."

"And just you or the staff operate it?"

"Yes." For the first time, a little heat crept into her tone. For some reason that encouraged Al, making him feel she was going to tough it through this. "You haven't asked me if anyone is missing from my regular or volunteer staff. They aren't, nor are any husbands, boyfriends, or whatever. That goes double for me since I don't have time in my life for anyone significant."

"Well, I'll still have to ask them all some questions."

"I understand." The steel gates had closed.

Al stood up. She was tired or a little pissed off. She'd had it. He'd gotten everything he could from her for the time being.

"From what you've said, I take it you're operating under the assumption that it was only one person's bones found." He watched her face crumble as he spoke.

"Oh, my Lord, do you mean...?"

"I'm afraid so," he said.

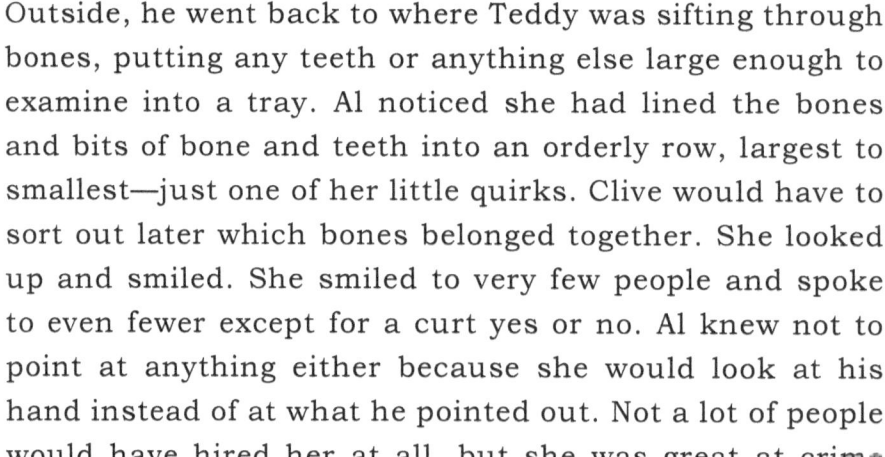

Outside, he went back to where Teddy was sifting through bones, putting any teeth or anything else large enough to examine into a tray. Al noticed she had lined the bones and bits of bone and teeth into an orderly row, largest to smallest—just one of her little quirks. Clive would have to sort out later which bones belonged together. She looked up and smiled. She smiled to very few people and spoke to even fewer except for a curt yes or no. Al knew not to point at anything either because she would look at his hand instead of at what he pointed out. Not a lot of people would have hired her at all, but she was great at crime scenes—thorough and not bothered by the proximity of death at all.

Clive was almost all the way inside the oven, raking out more ash and debris.

Al leaned inside the oven's mouth. "Will you be able to get DNA from these bones?" His words rattled in a low echo bouncing back from the far corners inside the oven.

"I'm guessing you know about the locus and DNA extraction methods, but these days we have a recent genetic marker system, STR, that's used with victims of fire or explosions. It can even help with paternity." Clive grinned back at Al. A larger soot streak stretched in a smear across the upper right corner of his forehead.

Al didn't say anything about the mark. He'd leave that to Teddy, who could be pretty candid about such things. She did speak to Clive. Al had caught her chattering away to him before, but she'd gone as quiet as a deepwater clam the moment he and Sheriff Clayton had entered the room.

"I'll follow up with the other employees and volunteers when they're back tomorrow," Al said. "Will you have everything you need from the site by then?"

"A crew is on their way here with lights and a few other hands. Teddy and I should have plenty to do all night. I was just wondering if the pizza places deliver out this far." Clive glanced up at where the afternoon sun was inching its way toward the horizon.

"I could ask Myra," Al said. "She probably knows."

"Ah, on a first-name basis already? You must take after your brother."

Al shook his head and turned to go, seeing no sense in responding. Maury was sure enough the womanizer of the pair—or had been until his heart attack. He probably would have returned to his ways if his nurse, Bonnie, hadn't kept a tight rein on him, occasionally wielding a small cast-iron skillet.

11

Taking a few steps, Al thought about the way Clive's Volvo was parked. He'd have had to jockey it around a few minutes to get it pointed that direction if he'd come in the way Al had.

Al turned around. "How did you get back here, Clive?"

"Back way. Quite by accident. There's no fence along the road and two lanes coming in. Turns out I took the back way. No biggie. It led me right to this little furnace."

Al took a few steps up the back lane, which stretched out in a straight line then doglegged at a sharp right angle near the end of the property to head for the road. He could make out a tangle of overlapping tire prints but no footprints in the packed dirt and gravel ruts of the drive. The land that stretched between him and the road hadn't experienced any landscaping touches yet. It had been cleared and maybe even plowed in the past but was covered in rough tufts of bunch grass and some patches of prickly pear cactus starts that were going to require someone to rent a backhoe to get rid of them. He saw no footprints or tire tracks going across the field.

Clive had backed his head out of the oven and was watching Al. He'd been to as many or more crime scenes than Al. "I doubt you need to spend much time with that. The human bones here didn't happen all at once. Some could be a week ago, others as much as a month ago. There's a lot to sort out here, but it's a bit of a cold case."

Al sighed and turned to head back past the shelter office and cages, toward his truck.

The dogs set up another eager chorus as he walked back out between the rows of cages—all of them, that is, except Tanner. Al paused to look down at the light-brown-and-white face, which still declined to beg. Al read the description: "Tanner, who is ten, came to the shelter when his owner just couldn't care for him anymore. He hasn't had even the smallest dustup with any of the other dogs. He promises to be a loving and not-too-demanding pet for anyone with a place in their home for a dog who follows his own muse and doesn't depend too much on others." Down in the lower right corner of the description was a three that had been marked out and a two penciled in. Tanner had two days to go.

Al looked down into the cage. Tanner looked back up at him with a resigned "it is what it is" look. Al stood there a couple more minutes, his feet feeling like lead holding him in place. He should be heading home. *Well, crap.* He supposed he was going to have to wade through some paperwork. He spun and started back toward the shelter's front door.

During the drive back to his place, the sky had darkened. Al turned on his lights and glanced toward the passenger seat. Tanner sat on his haunches, looking out the window. He glanced toward Al as if sensing his attention.

"You're not going to be any kind of problem, are you?" Al said.

Tanner tilted his head and gave Al the best look Al could hope for, the one that said, *"Look, I don't intend to be in the way at all. You'll hardly notice I'm around unless you want me to be."* Tanner had yet to bark or whine once.

Al pulled into the parking lot of the only pet-supply shop he knew of on the way home. From his pocket, he took the list Myra had written for him, including what kind of food would be best for Tanner, as well as a few chew toys and treats.

"Nobody ever got me any chew toys or treats," Al said. "Are you going to be okay in here by yourself for a few minutes?"

Tanner gave him the look, as patient and as unflinching as the Sphinx. *"You can count on me."*

When Al came back out to his truck with a thirty-pound bag of dog food over his shoulder and a sack full of chew toys, treats, and a dog's water-and-food dish, Tanner was sitting in the same spot and didn't even try to shoot out the door when Al opened it.

He put the supplies behind his seat. "Myra said that of all the kinds of food that get donated to the shelter, this one seemed to be your favorite brand. Is that okay with you?"

Tanner looked back, the small beginning of a grin on his patient and serious face.

Before he started the truck, Al reached back into the sack and took out a small plastic beefsteak or pork chop. Whatever it was, it squeaked. He held it out to Tanner.

"You've been pretty good so far. Do you want this for the rest of the trip?"

Tanner looked up at Al, down at the toy, up at Al, and down at the toy again. He couldn't seem to believe it. *"For me?"* He leaned cautiously forward, opened his mouth, and closed it ever so gently on the toy, which barely gave a slow squeak. He turned and looked forward, ready to go.

As he drove through the growing dark, Al glanced at Tanner from time to time. The dog sat still with the toy held in his mouth, not chewing, just hanging onto it as if it was the first thing he'd ever been given in his life. He ignored the road and what passed by beyond the windows and just stared at Al.

"Now, tomorrow, I have to go back out and ask a lot of people some tomfool questions. Are you going to be all right while I'm gone?" Al said.

Tanner looked back as if saying, *"Everything is going to be just fine. Just fine."*

Al nodded and turned back to the road, telling himself that everything was indeed going to be fine. He wished he could hold onto that slippery notion.

The picture of Teddy so neatly lining up those bits of bones and teeth from a number of humans on the tray came back into sharp focus, and the cynicism of twenty-five years of Murphy's Law in the sheriff's department kicked in. Al suspected—a niggling, gnawing suspicion—that, at least as far as the case went, everything *wasn't* going to be just fine. And his gut was usually right about such things.

CHAPTER TWO

AL DROVE PAST THE OLD hollowed-out shell of the Springer place. His headlights swept across the stone chimney sticking up out of the ground like a monument to where the burned-down cabin used to be. The landmark told him he was within a mile of his house. As usually happened when he knew he was heading home, he found himself going slightly faster than he intended—the horse smelling the barn. He eased up on the accelerator. The sky surrounding his truck darkened in earnest, the way it would on most Texas nights, like someone pulling on a cord to turn out the lights. Tanner had been quiet the whole way, watching Al more than the countryside rolling along outside the passenger window. He still held his chew toy in his mouth, his grip soft enough that it only let out a slow squeak from time to time.

Al used the time driving to mull over the details of the crime scene. Well, it wasn't so much a crime scene as a body dump. He was chewing that over in his mind, slowly at first but a little more vigorously than Tanner was having at his toy, when an idea came to him. He slowed the truck, looked around, and made a U-turn to head back the way he'd come. Tanner tilted his head.

"Yeah, I wanted to be home too, but sometimes, we don't have much of a choice about these things." He dug out his cell phone and hit a speed-dial number.

Julie Ann was still on her shift as dispatcher and answered. "Yeah? What'ya want, Al?"

"Clive and the crime-scene crew are still at that dog shelter, aren't they?"

"Yep."

"Could you do me a favor and look up any more shelters like that, just outside the city limits, the way this one was? Just the ones with an on-site incinerator. Call and ask if you have to."

"Okey-dokey."

"Text me a list of what you find. Oh, and copy Clive on the text too."

"Clayton too?"

"We won't rouse that sleeping bear unless we have more than a hunch."

"He's standing right here beside me. Doesn't look like he's hibernating. Want me to give him a nudge?"

"Nope."

Al hung up quickly and closed the flip-phone. "Might not have scored many points with the boss just then," he told Tanner, "but I'm already retired. What's he gonna do, fire me?"

Tanner shuffled a front paw and gave Al his first worried look. His mouth drooped, and his eyes grew sad. *Maybe he was picking up on vibes.* Years had passed since Al had owned a dog or even been around one much. He recalled they all seemed to have their own personalities, and some were smarter than others, more intuitive. Tanner, though, was a little hard to figure out. One of the first clues to anyone's personality, Al always thought, was to know what the person wanted. Right then, Tanner looked as though he had everything he'd ever wanted and was a little overwhelmed and distrustful of that. He couldn't believe his good luck and wasn't going to do a thing to spoil it.

The area behind the shelter was lit by the bright generator-driven lights, which made it look like a landing site for aliens. The white of the lights was bright enough to have a keen edge to it, casting a ghostly pale aurora borealis of an aura against the black sky. Al could hear the dogs barking, stirred up by the crime-scene crew tromping around. Most nights were probably calmer out there, perhaps with an occasional coyote trotting too close. The lights and movements had whipped some of the dogs into a frenzy. Al heard a low whimper and looked down. Tanner's eyes had gotten huge, and he was trembling.

"Hey, little fellow. I guess you know where you are. I'm not taking you back to the shelter. Okay?"

Al pulled up behind a van and turned off his motor. He reached behind the seats and got the bag from the pet store. He opened the box of treats, removed one, and held it out to Tanner, who didn't let go of his toy but quivered harder. Al put the treat down beside Tanner's paw, but the dog's eyes stayed fixed on Al.

"I get it. You're scared. You think I'm turning you back in. Don't be. I'm not. Just stay here, and I'll be right back as soon as I can."

He closed his door, and Tanner moved across to press against the glass and watch Al walk away as he headed toward the bright lights. He passed a crime-scene worker, Clarence, a younger black man newer to the group. Clarence looked up, shared half a quick wave, and shook his head. Well, Al hadn't expected much, anything like footprints or tire markings they could use. The scene was cold, but they would be thorough. Clayton would expect nothing less.

Clive looked up as Al drew near. Teddy had moved closer to Clive. She didn't mind dead bodies, but the hubbub of all the people around usually made her a bit twitchy. Al had seen her tighten before, avoiding eye contact altogether and drawing into herself. She reached to straighten the row of bones in the tray.

"I thought we'd done about all we can and were going to get to go home, Al," Clive said. "What do you have?"

"A hunch." Al took out his cell phone.

Julie Ann had sent the list. He'd heard the message ping in.

"I got it too," Clive said. "A while ago. Had time to mull it over. Are you going where I think you're headed?"

"I'm afraid so, Clive." Al looked around. The crime-scene crew was running into a dead end. The scene was cold. He'd expected that.

"So, what do we do?" Clive stood up, brushing ash off the front of his pant legs.

"If this is a body dump and the bones are from several people, then chances are we're at the tip of something a whole lot bigger. You can sort out what you can at the lab. But I think we might look at a few of these similar places." He tapped the screen of his cell phone.

"Right now?"

"Yep. Before someone gets the notion to clean them ahead of us."

"All of them?"

"Pick one," Al said. "Someplace likely, equidistant to the city or the center of whatever activity is leading to the deaths."

"I notice you've avoided the big places in the city. You think the next place you'll find will be isolated, like this one. Right?"

Al nodded.

Teddy looked up at Al and managed half a smile. She knew and trusted him, but the noise of the rest of the crew nosing around crowded her, and she stiffened, turning back to the comfort of arranging the row of bones.

"There's a place on the list, a private kennel and shelter, not far from where I live," Clive said. "I know they have a furnace not too different from this one. We can call ahead, alert the owner. We could be in and out, have a quick answer for you. Will that calm your jets?"

"It will if we don't find more human bones," Al said.

"I hope we don't," Clive said.

"Me too," Al said.

Back at the truck, Tanner moved back to the passenger side as Al slid into his seat. Tanner was still softly mouthing his chew-toy security blanket. The treat lay untasted by Tanner's paw.

Al held out a hand and cupped Tanner's head. It was quivering, and Tanner pressed back against Al's hand.

"There, you see?" Al said. "We're going to get out of here and not leave you back there again. That okay with you?"

Tanner's eyes brightened, and for the first time, his tail rose, and he gave a couple of quick wags.

———◆———

Al pulled into a mom-and-pop convenience store on his way to the next shelter and got a big cup of coffee and a package of beef jerky. He'd skipped supper, and hard to tell how long checking out the next site would take. A fishing buddy of his, Bubba Ray James, liked to call beef jerky a redneck wonder food. According to its manufacturer, that particular package contained beef, sugar, water, salt, some kind of soy, and what looked like half a dozen different chemical ways of saying good old sodium. He'd rather have had a plate of sashimi at his favorite sushi bar, but for the moment, he was on the "Bubba likes it" plan.

Back in the truck, he took a sip of the black coffee and

put the cup in the holder. Then he tore open the package and took a bite of beef jerky before starting the truck. Tanner's ears rose. He stared at Al then slowly lowered his chew toy to the seat and let it drop. He licked his lips and stared at Al.

"Oh, I get it... subtle as you are." Al broke off a small piece and held it out.

Tanner licked it out of his fingers and chewed slowly, savoring, his eyes bright and his tail whipping back and forth with the most vigor Al had seen yet. Al pulled out of the lot and drove toward the next pet shelter, where he'd agreed to meet Clive. He gave Tanner only a couple more small pieces. He didn't want to come back to the truck and find Tanner throwing up. When Tanner saw Al was done and was not going to share any more, he sniffed around, found the treat from earlier, ate that, then picked up his chew toy and looked ahead through the windshield as the truck wove through the county roads through a largely sleeping population, or at least curled up on the couch in front of the TV.

Al had given Clive time to get to the shelter first, and the silver Volvo was parked out front. Clive came out the front door of the shelter, accompanied by a lanky redheaded young man whose tousled hair and blinking eyes hinted that Clive might have roused him. Maybe the fellow had gone to bed early since he had to get up and open early or do chores.

Al often sketched out a quick life story in his head when meeting someone, then watched the person's character flesh out, to see how close he'd been. That guy looked like someone who probably loved animals and wanted to do great good in his world then found the work was a whole lot more thankless than he'd expected, but by damn he was going to stick it out and get the job done even if it

21

wasn't everything he'd expected. That showed purpose and resolve but left out whether anyone else was still sleeping in the house and was part of making the guy's life less lonely while on his particular mission.

Compared to those at the previous shelter, the dogs were not barking quite as frantically. The place was a kennel as well. That didn't mean all the dogs were better behaved, but they did sound less desperate.

"This is Taylor." Clive waved a hand holding a long flashlight toward the lanky redhead. "Taylor James."

Al shook hands, a curt, dry shake. He guessed Taylor gave the dogs more personal attention than humans. "Do you run the place by yourself?" Al looked around at what he could see of the rescue center.

"Mostly. It's the only way the place pays. I have a few volunteers, but I get the joy of most of the work myself." He rubbed a hand over his face, still getting the sleep out of his eyes, and grinned.

"Let's get this over with, and maybe I can recall what being between covers feels like," Clive said.

Teddy got out of the Volvo and took a rake, a bucket, and a trowel out of the back end. She hurried up to them, and they all headed off, none of them trying to speak as the chorus of yips, barks, and yowls increased around them. Teddy kept her head down. Al could tell she was tuckered, but she was a trouper and would walk all night through fire if that were where Clive was headed. He suspected she'd had a rough childhood, but finding someone who respected her and treated her as an equal seemed to have motivated her to great deeds. He'd seen her working at Clive's lab before, and she did the work of two people and seemed delighted to have the opportunity to do it.

"Do you use the furnace much?" Al asked.

"Rarely." Taylor frowned. "Haven't in six months."

Al started to feel that sinking in his stomach. *Maybe this was a bad choice. Well, we're here.*

Clive moved closer to Al, keeping his voice low. "Are you going to tell me your hunch, Al?"

"Let's just wait and see. Okay?"

"Anyone but you, Al, and I'd tell them to take a flying jump. But I've known you far too long, and you've been right far more often than the average bear."

The furnace was different from the one at the other shelter. It was newer and looked far less used. Its metal sides still shone silver, and it was nestled inside a tall cedar fence that kept it hidden on three sides yet was far enough away not to catch fire.

"How come only a few shelters even have furnaces, Taylor?" Al had a notion but wanted to hear it from the shelter owner.

Taylor's mouth twisted up at the corner. "Because it's expensive, the most expensive way there is to dispose of the bodies. But I tend to think it's the most dignified. Damn thing set me back a bit, and it's the least-used part of the place. I hope to be able to keep it that way."

"What are the other ways to go? I mean with the bodies of euthanized pets."

"Well, the cheapest is to call some guys I know with a truck. They pick up the bodies and don't charge me a thing."

"How can they afford to do that?"

"They get their money from a rendering plant. You know, Lassie becomes tallow, meat, and blood byproducts—and even hair byproducts—turned into things people buy, everyday products people use for a lot of things, even for their animals. All you have to do is read some labels of products and look for words like *hydrolyzed animal protein, blood meal, bone meal, meat byproducts, tallow,* and that sort of thing. No pet that's ever been under my roof will ever go that way."

"And that's it, the choice, the fork in the road?"

"Well, in some places, there's the landfill. I followed the big Austin center's effort to maintain a 'no kill' pet shelter, but even they wanted a pet incinerator. As far as using landfills here, I haven't even explored that direction. Call me fussy. I paid for this damn thing"—he waved a hand toward the furnace—"but, as I said, it's been quite a while since I fired it up at all."

Clive was pulling on his gloves. He glanced toward Al then reached and swung the door open. "Oh, damn."

"What?" Taylor crowded closer.

"You sure you haven't fired this up in the past couple of weeks?"

"Sure, I'm sure. Why?"

"Well, someone has. Maybe more recently than that, too. Teddy, hand me that rake if you will."

Clive drew a clump of ashy shards close. Al could make out the curve of part of a skull. Some of the jawline remained, showing three back teeth. Clive looked up at Al.

Taylor pressed closer, going up on his toes to peer over Clive's shoulder. When he could make out what he was seeing and knew it for what it was, he spun and staggered off a few steps, bent at the knees, and vomited.

Clive stepped back, and Teddy eased in, moving the pile of ash at the back of the furnace closer to the front. Al wasn't sure of her pathology, just how much autism or whatever she had, but bones of dead people didn't bother her the way crowds of living people did. She was fine with that chore. *Go figure.* She kept at it while Clive and Al moved a few steps away from the furnace and away from Taylor, who was still bent at the waist and had a firm grip on his own knees.

"More than one set of bones?" Al asked.

"Too soon to tell, but if your hunch is on, probably."

"Is there a way to tell ethnicity from bones burned this bad?"

"Sure, if there's enough to go on. The skull will help, for sure. A Caucasian victim will have a narrower face and high-bridged nasal bone. The upper incisors should have a flat lingual surface. The chin will often be more prominent and the cheekbones flat. A black person's skull often has a broader nose bridge with wider nasal openings, subnasal grooves, and the skull may have outward-sloping jaws. I'm gonna make a suggestion here, Al. Let's not send this out into the system just yet and take a chance the feds get a whiff. I've got an anthropologist pal on campus. Of the stone-and-bone folks, he's a bone guy. Just for chuckles, let's get his take first. What's the rest of your hunch?"

"I'm thinking we'll find Asian or Hispanic. If this is really messed up, maybe some of both."

"The can of worms we're dancing around, then, is human trafficking. Right?"

Al nodded. "Just don't breathe a word of that yet anywhere until we're absolutely sure and have had a chance to nose around on our own first. You hear?"

"You don't have to tell me. That's exactly why I want to go to my local bones guy first. Well, I'd better call the crime-scene people and move them over here. This site is a whole lot fresher. You might as well go home and sleep. You're gonna have to question a whole lot more people tomorrow."

Al looked down at the small pile of bones Teddy was getting out of the furnace. Everyone there could look forward to a long night of thrashing about, making sure they missed nothing that might tell them what had transpired. He headed toward his truck. After having worked far too many similar sites alone, he appreciated the company and the relieved look Tanner shared when Al got back to the truck, slid into his seat, and asked, "What do you say we head home now?"

Tanner's tail gave a couple of quick wags, and he sat up and looked ahead as Al pulled out and they rolled off through the night.

CHAPTER THREE

Bonnie's watch showed 5:47 a.m. as she climbed up the stairs from the basement room Al called his guest quarters. *Early, but what the heck? That's what comes of going to bed at 9 p.m. When she was done sleeping, she was done.* That was the way she was. Fergie, Al's former high-school classmate and her current roommate downstairs, was the same way. She was in the shower downstairs right then. Bonnie had already showered and dressed. She'd found it best not to wear just pajamas and a robe upstairs since Maury was sleeping on the living-room couch. He was apt to pounce like some jungle beast. Even though she always got the best of him, his amorous attacks could be nerve-wracking some mornings. She'd even thought of slipping some saltpeter into his food, something to tone down that propensity of his. Just when she thought she'd tamed him, she would look up to see him peering in from outside the shower. The last time that had happened, Fergie was the one who caught him and frog-stepped him up the stairs while giving him the usual lecture and occasional knee to the rear all the way up. However, Maury was Maury, with the skin of a rhino, and so unlike Al, whom she wouldn't mind stirring into a little of that sort of enthusiasm.

Maury still formed a sleeping, blanket-covered lump on the couch as she skirted past him on her way to the kitchen. In the quiet of the hour, the wooden house seemed to breathe in time to the breeze coming off the adjacent lake. A limb of a live oak that needed trimming scraped against the outside of the upper floor.

Once in the kitchen, she flipped on the lights. She liked that room, with its brown Spanish tiles, granite counters, and knotty-pine-paneled walls, with the lake right outside, though she couldn't see it in the dark squares of the windows at that hour. She was reaching for the canister of coffee beans when she saw a two-part bowl on the floor with water and dog food.

"Well, that's new," she said.

At nearly 8:00 a.m., Bonnie and Fergie were sitting at the table with empty bowls in front of them when Al came out of his bedroom with Tanner trotting along at his heel.

Bonnie saw the little brown-and-white dog first.

"Oh, isn't he the sweetest-looking little thing?" She got out of her chair, sank to her haunches, and held out a hand, fingers down.

"His name is Tanner," Al said.

Tanner looked up at him then eased close to Bonnie's hand to give it a sniff and a small, tentative lick. He looked up at her with soulful and cautious brown eyes, and she thought her heart was going to split in two.

"He's a rescue dog," Al said as he poured himself a cup of coffee from the thermos. "He didn't have much time left."

Bonnie could've sworn she heard a tiny catch in Al's voice.

One corner of Fergie's mouth twitched up. Where Bonnie was barely over five feet tall and had curly blond hair and a figure Maury had described as dumplingesque, Fergie was six foot two and lanky, and her long red hair swept down over shoulders that suggested she still did push-ups as well as a whole exercise regime. She was the same age as Al, and Bonnie thought it irked him that she looked only half as old.

Bonnie rubbed Tanner's head then slid her hand under his chin and rubbed. He tilted his head and half closed his eyes as if to say, *"Yeah, that's the spot."*

"You know, it could be you getting a morning petting, Al," Bonnie said. "You just need to loosen up and decide which one of us you want to move in upstairs with you." She winked at Fergie.

Al, who had just taken a gulp of coffee, nearly shot it back out his nose.

"There's some oatmeal in the pot," Bonnie said. "It's what Fergie and I had." As she said it, she fought the notion of seeing oatmeal trying to make its way in a burst through his nasal passages.

He shook his head no.

"You were out late last night," Fergie said. "I thought you had just a quick hop out to see about some bones that might be human."

"It turned out to be a little more complicated than that."

"Hey, don't let him off the hook, String Bean. I was just getting him to squirm good." Bonnie dug her fingers harder into Tanner's back, which he arched as he wagged his tail and rolled his eyes back.

"Heaven." He was probably having a hard time realizing he'd been sitting ignored in a kennel cage just a day before.

"I'm no string bean, as Al can attest." Fergie winked at Al. Two pink flushed spots appeared on his cheekbones. "Though he knows all your features too when you sneak into bed so he can wake to find you naked there. It's a good thing Sheriff Clayton doesn't know anything about Al's home life, or he'd think Al was living somewhere between Woodstock and the last days of Caligula."

"I wonder myself, some days," Al muttered.

"Hey, don't let him kid you," Bonnie said. "He doesn't jump right out of the bed when he realizes I'm snuggled up naked against him. He enjoys the spooning as much as I do."

Al finished his coffee and put his mug down. "As much fun as this is, I've got to go. Can either or both of you keep an eye on Tanner today? I shouldn't be at this too much longer. Clayton says he's gonna pick a new detective to train real soon."

"Hey, did I hear someone say the word *naked* in here? I'm right in the other room, you know, trying to sleep." Maury finished tying the belt of his plaid robe and reached up to scratch his tousled hair.

"I'm out of here before this conversation goes any farther," Al said.

"If you're not taking any pay, why don't they let Fergie be your partner?" Maury said. "She's been a detective before."

"I'm not taking pay because I'm doing the department a favor."

"Plus, you can walk away whenever you want, and they can't boss you," Bonnie said.

"Where'd the dog come from?" Maury asked. He squatted on his haunches and massaged Tanner with both hands, making the dog's eyes roll.

As Al headed to the door, Tanner looked up at Al with sad eyes and started to follow, but Fergie got down on her knees and started rubbing him, too. The dog peered up at Al with torn emotions. Al was clearly his guy, but Tanner had four hands on him right then—four, all petting away after weeks at the shelter. Still, as joyous as that might have felt, he managed to wrench himself away and take tentative steps until he stood looking up at Al with soulful eyes that seemed to get bigger.

"I understand," Al told him. "But I need you to guard the whole lot of these loonies for now. Okay?" He spun and started for the door then paused and came back.

Tanner stood frozen in one spot, looking up at him, a little dazed and confused at the prospect of being apart for the first time. Al got down on one knee and rubbed Tanner's head. "I'm asking a big favor of you, Tanner. Understand? It's a responsibility. While you're here, I want you to watch over these ladies and even Maury. It's a big job, but I'm counting on you. Will you do it?"

When he rose, Tanner stood still, looking up with the saddest eyes Bonnie had seen yet. From the look on Al's face, Bonnie figured he was right on the edge too and about to get all sloppy emotional or something.

"Well, okay," Al said. "Maybe it's too soon. Don't want you to feel abandoned. You can come." *Some big, tough cop I am.*

Tanner shot across the room like a furry little lightning bolt. Al grabbed Tanner's leash on the way out, and a second later, the door closed behind the two of them, a real Mutt and Jeff pair if Bonnie had ever seen one.

"He's a hard man to figure," Fergie said. "Soft. And hard."

Maury was tugging on his slippers. He retightened the belt on his robe and raced to the door.

Bonnie heard Al's truck start. "Yeah, but when he's hard, he's real hard." She caught Fergie staring at her. "I meant in a fight."

"Sure you did," Fergie said. "Sure you did."

Al had barely turned the key and let the motor warm for

a second when the front door of the house flew open and Maury came running toward the truck, still wearing his robe, the belt ends flapping behind him.

"What's the matter?" Al asked.

Maury opened the passenger door and slid in, closing the door behind him. Tanner hopped off the passenger seat and got under Al's legs.

"I just wanted to talk. Okay?"

"What's on your mind?"

"Have you made a decision, Al?"

"About what?"

"About which of them you want?"

"What are you talking about?"

"Fergie and Bonnie. What else?"

"I've had other things on my mind. You know that. The sheriff has a clutter of cases that need cleaned up. He's short-handed, and I just found that the web of one of them is more tangled than we'd hoped."

"Yet you find time to come home with a dog. Nice little guy, actually. I'll bet *he* spent the night on your bed with you."

"He stayed on the floor, curled up on the rug like a little watchdog determined nobody was going to get to me."

"I see. Helping you play hard to get."

"I'm not playing. I *am* hard to get. Now, what's really on your mind?" Al watched Maury's face, catching little telltale tics, nervous twitches that said he hadn't gotten to his real agenda yet.

"Well, you know how I keep an eye on the obituaries where we grew up?"

"Yeah. As hobbies go, it's a little... well, odd." He doubted Maury was—well, hoped he wasn't—the type to gloat about being alive while others his age weren't.

"Your roommate from college, before you lived with Abbie... Well, he's dead."

32

"Kevin? What from? He was two years younger than me."

"It didn't say. But you know how Kevin was, kind of burning his candle at both ends all the time."

"Yeah, Kevin Beale, the only guy able to make *you* look like a slow mover where women were concerned."

"A real horndog," Maury said. "A champion." A touch of admiration showed in his voice.

"Did you know he went on to become a top salesman of medical supplies? He had that ready smile, a killer dimple, and was a real closer. When we roomed together, he would sometimes show up with one girl for a date at home, send her on her way, and go get another. In the morning, yet another would come out from his room."

"What a guy," Maury said.

Al shook his head. "I kept in touch with Kevin for a while. We shared one or two beers. Then, we both drifted off and apart. Didn't have that much in common. But damn, I am sorry to hear that."

"I thought you'd want to know."

"Thanks, I guess. I hadn't heard. But why the rush out here to tell me?"

"I knew you'd care. But there's the other thing."

"What other thing?"

"You know, guy a couple of years younger than you kicks off like that, and here you are taking chances."

"Chances?"

"Are you sure what you're doing is the right thing? Is this what you want to be doing? The last couple of times came darn close to killing you. Is this really how you saw yourself spending your time?" Maury looked at Al then looked away. He reached down to hold a hand out to Tanner, who licked it but stayed close to Al's leg.

"So, this is really your way of letting me know you worry about me?"

"Well, yeah. I guess so." Maury stared into Al's eyes with a shared intensity Al hadn't felt from him in a long time. "It's just that I've also seen a side of you I'd never seen. You can be the softest, most warmhearted guy I know. But when you get your back up all the way, I saw you snuff out guys bigger than you, younger than you, who should have been stronger and faster than you. You were a cobra, and you took them out without a look back. It gives me the willies, if you want to know. You let that keep growing, where are you?"

"I've thought about that, Maury, but I can't be half of what I am. I've had training, and I know my limitations and even how to edge past them when I'm really up against it. I don't enjoy some of what I have to do, but I don't back down from it, either. It's part of the job, and when push comes to shove, I've always loved the job."

"You know, once I didn't think much about what our final days would be like, how we'd spend our time." Maury looked down at his slippers then back up again at Al. "Now, I just hope you're around to spend them with."

"That's a kind thing to say. I hope that too." Al didn't feel the need to touch on how Maury had been a half a step away from Al breaking his neck once. His marriage with Abbie having been wrecked—by Maury—Al had made himself stay away, and he and Maury hadn't spoken in twenty years until just a short while ago. *At least all that was behind them.* Well, he hoped it was.

Maury slipped out of the truck and slumped off toward the house. Al glanced at his watch. *Well, he'd better scoot and make up some time now.* Tanner hopped back onto the passenger seat, ready to go. He glanced at Al with what Al took for a knowing look.

"Yeah, I suppose you have family somewhere, too," Al said to Tanner.

Ma Wee started down the concrete stairway at the side of the crumbling building, its older-style architecture hinting it had once been some sort of postal building or a Masonic hall. Not many Texas buildings had basements; they were built on concrete slabs instead. It sat alone at the end of a row of warehouses next to chain-link-fenced scrap and wrecking yards. Someone had hunkered down on the stairs as a place to stay at night. A row of beer cans sat along the edge of two steps. From the aroma, she guessed a few of the cans had served as a restroom to someone who didn't want to move once he'd settled in. Something black, which she hoped was a roach, shot wriggling into a crack near the bottom of the stairs. She'd been taken to worse places, but not many. An airplane roared not far away as it backed its brakes in a landing.

She heard the sound of a car pull up and looked back up behind her, unable to see the vehicle, but the head of the driver appeared. He nodded and started down the steps after her. He was not a big man, but she was small. She reached out and opened the building's door.

The room inside was brightly lit. Fluorescent panels of lights hanging across the ceiling were all on. The inside of the building was cleaner than the stairway, but not much. The basement was empty except for a shiny steel table on the far end of the room beside a pair of deep porcelain sinks. A man she didn't know stood in front of one of the sinks, his back to her. She heard the sound of water running.

Ma Wee stopped just inside the door and lowered her suitcase to the floor.

"Did you take care of all your good-byes? Ready to leave that part of your life behind you?" His voice was deep, stentorian, a man of some considerable authority.

"Yes." Her voice trembled like a leaf. She could remember all the way back to being much younger and hungry in Bangkok, a burden to her parents and three brothers and two sisters. The man she'd met twenty years before had said he would pay to send her to America and to get her papers, and she would have a job in a restaurant when she arrived. That had sounded too good to be true. Too good to be true. It had been.

"Do you have the passport for me you promised?" she asked.

"Of course."

He dried his hands on a brown paper towel torn off a roll. She hadn't expected to be taken there—a bus station or the airport, but not to a crumbling building on the edge of town. At least it was in the direction of the airport. She didn't know how long the process of being set free would take. She was eager to go, to get out of there. They'd said she could go, at last.

She had recently turned thirty-six and still had some good years ahead. She'd looked at herself in the mirror before leaving her tiny room, one she was glad enough to leave behind. The face in the glass still showed the traces of her as a scared, skinny girl, but she had a few lines, a few gray hairs beginning, which she could always dye black. But she would be free, at last. Others had left, and they'd not come back. She didn't plan to come back, either. *Just a short while longer. She could stand it.*

An arm that came from behind her pressed and held a cloth to her nose and mouth, the other arm wrapping around her and clasping her in place. The smell that engulfed her senses was noxious, like alcohol and cleaning products combined.

She began to feel woozy, tried to kick backward, but her foot was heavy, so heavy. She could barely lift it. The sound of someone's feet shuffling in the room grew muffled. Everything went hazy then black.

CHAPTER FOUR

ON THEIR MORNING DRIVE, TANNER sat squarely in the center of the passenger seat, his alert head looking forward, only now and then glancing out his passenger window. His new red leash lay in a coil by one paw. They went past a small lake, a shiny skin of orange-and-yellow light where the sun washed its smooth surface, dotted by rings made by fish feeding. Most of the traffic was heading toward the city. Al was glad to peel off and turn in to the second shelter where they'd found human bones.

The crime-scene crew had turned off the generator and were almost done taking down the light stands that had lit the area in a surface-of-the-moon white. Al pulled up behind Clive's silver Volvo station wagon and turned off his engine.

"You're going to have to stay close to me here," Al said. He turned to Tanner, who sat looking up at him with his leash in his mouth. "Way ahead of me, aren't you?" He rubbed Tanner's head and clipped on the leash.

He opened his door, and Tanner sprang across the seats in little bounds and leaped to the ground, shook himself, and looked around.

Al thought Tanner might tense up near a shelter, but the other dogs were quiet for the moment after a night of disruption, and Tanner seemed to know it wasn't the same shelter where he'd been waiting in a cage. They took off with Tanner high-stepping along beside Al. He set a brisk little pace that matched Al's stride, not zooming ahead of him, content to be side by side.

The first person Al saw was Clarence, who was wearing his Crime Scene ball cap so the bill stuck out to one side. He was coiling up stretches of power cords for the lights and stood by an almost full box of the coils.

"Did you know your hat's on sideways, Clarence?" Al said.

Clarence reached up to turn the bill forward. "Back when I'm at home, it's the way I wear it."

"No worries. I'm not busting your chops. I don't care if that's how you do it in the hood, or here for that matter," Al said. "I was just afraid it was going to lead you to walk sideways and bonk into something."

"Oh, you think you jest, but I'm tired enough for that. We all are."

"Do you think you found anything?"

"My gut says no. I've been doing this long enough for that. I got a few footprints and tire tracks, but a glance at the vehicles and shoes that belong here tell me I won't have much that's new, if anything. Nice dog." He bent down to pet Tanner, who let him.

"Where's Clive?"

"Over going through the ashes one last time before he boogies out of here, too."

Al headed toward the oven and saw Clive sitting on the front end of the incinerator staring off at nothing.

"You okay, Clive?"

The ME looked up, saw it was Al, and nodded.

"You look like you've been shot out of the wrong end of a cannon," Al said.

"You mean there's a right end?"

"You should go home." Al nodded toward Clive's Volvo.

"I'm working up the energy to get to the car," Clive said. "We're all wrapped up here. I was making sure we missed nothing."

"Clayton will be glad."

"You'd think so. He called to say he wants us to check the other pet shelters with incinerators or anything like them."

"Oh. Where's Teddy?"

"Asleep in the backseat of the Volvo. That's where I should be too." He hesitated. "I mean, not with Teddy, but by myself. Alone in my own bed at home."

Al did a pretty good job of suppressing a smile. "You're tired. I get it. How about this? Maybe I can get him to tape off the other spots and put a watch on each until you and the others have had time to catch up on sleep."

"That would be a lifesaver, Al."

Tanner was sniffing at Clive's pant leg, so Clive reached down to scratch Tanner behind the ears. Tanner tilted his head and closed his eyes.

Clive creaked back upright while Tanner moved closer to the incinerator and sniffed around its base.

"Don't ever get old, Al," Clive said.

"Aren't we about the same age?"

"Yeah, but at least you had the sense to retire."

"Fat lot of good it's doing me."

Al heard a squeal and turned to see Teddy clamber out of the open back door of Clive's Volvo. She left the door open and came running. As soon as she was near them, she squatted beside Tanner and held out her hands. Tanner glanced up to Al then moved closer. Teddy lifted him and hugged him to her chest. He looked over her shoulder at Al, and if dogs could shrug, Al was pretty sure that was what Tanner did.

Teddy lowered him to the ground and turned to Al. She held out a hand. "Walk?"

Al knew what a chore words were for Teddy at times. "Sure. I guess, if it's okay with Tanner." He held out the loop end of the leash, and Teddy started off with Tanner, both going at a brisk walk.

"They shouldn't be long," Al said to Clive.

"That's okay. She needs this. Been around too many people. I'm told they're using dogs a lot now with autistic people. It calms them tremendously when they're stressed. Poor Teddy was close to an overdose of other people." Clive watched the two of them as they got farther away.

Al was watching too and saw Tanner tugging to his left. That wasn't like him. At first, Teddy tugged back, but then she gave him his lead, and he took off at a run with her running along behind.

"Now where is she going?" Clive said.

"Clarence!" Al yelled. To Clive, he lowered his voice and said, "Don't hop into your car just yet. I think Tanner's onto something." When Clarence came running up, Al pointed in the direction Teddy and Tanner were headed. "What's off that way?"

"I don't know. We didn't get that far. We had plenty to do here."

"Well, you'd better come along and take a look." Al took off at a jog, and the much younger and clearly more athletically fit Clarence was soon right beside him.

Teddy and Tanner trotted along ahead of them, and Al thought he heard Teddy giggle, something he'd never heard her do before.

He glanced back, and the shelter seemed a good distance away. They were almost to the far end of the field when Al saw a small dirt road that ran in two brown ruts along the other side of a fence.

41

"Teddy," he yelled. "Hold up."

Teddy had to pull on Tanner's leash, but he slowed and turned until Al and Clarence caught up. Al was huffing, but Clarence looked as unruffled by the run as he'd been before they started. Al bent to grab his knees, and Tanner came running over.

"New scene to check out." Al huffed. He waved one hand at the road. "This is how someone could get in and out of the place."

Clarence nodded. He took off at an even faster run back toward the shelter to get his equipment and some help. Al liked the aspect of Clarence that leaped to do things right, even when he'd been up all night staring at beaten-up half footprints in bad lighting.

Tanner climbed up Al's shin to lick the back of his hand. Teddy dropped down into a squat beside Tanner to pet him. She was wearing the happiest smile Al had ever seen on her. Maybe Clive was right about stress, though that didn't seem to be the case with Clive. His face hung as tired and droopy as a Salvador Dali clock as he trudged across the field to catch up with them. Clarence walked beside him, carrying his kit, which looked like a large tackle box.

"I'll call Clayton," Al said. "I'm fresh and can work the crime scene. You and Teddy need to take a break. Okay?"

"I'm good for another shift if you need a hand, Al," Clarence said.

"You're on." Al turned to the ME. "I mean it, Clive. You've done your bit. We'll fence off the other shelters and work this lead while you catch up with the sandman."

"Al, I believe I'll name my next child after you."

Al didn't remind him that, moments before, Clive had admitted he was Al's age, and Al knew no children were in his own future.

Teddy smiled and gave Tanner one more pat and rose to head off with Clive.

Tanner looked up at Al and wagged his tail.

"Well, you do work wonders," Al said. "I believe if we could bottle whatever it is you have, Tanner, we might just whip this autism thing."

Al climbed over the three-strand barbed-wire fence, carrying Tanner. He set him down on the other side but held him back until Clarence could join them.

The field on the other side of the fence had been allowed to go fallow. The green was almost knee deep, dotted with white-and-yellow blooms that extended all the way to a copse of trees that grew thicker as it went up a gradual then steeper hill.

His heart was hammering at an accelerated but happy rhythm. What Al hadn't told Maury in their little talk was that this was what he missed: the puzzle-solving, figuring things out, the chase, and the attempt to put an orderly world in place where there was chaos and confusion. He hadn't been successful every time. No one had. However, rather than fretting over the dangers Maury had hinted at, he savored such moments.

Clarence climbed over the fence, pausing only once to free his pants from one of the barbs. Al loosened his grip on Tanner's leash enough that the little fellow could tug him in a direction. Tire prints pressed into the dirt ruts. At a low spot in the fence where Tanner seemed determined to haul him, Al spotted footprints too. The thrill of whatever made Al wish to hunt and find things tingled through him.

"Here you go, Clarence. Footprints."

Clarence came running. "Great. Good clear ones."

"And these are the ones that interested Tanner from the scent he picked up over at the incinerator."

"Sweet. Maybe now we're getting somewhere."

Al kept Tanner back away from the area by crouching down and petting him while Clarence got to work marking where he wanted to take impressions.

Clarence had some of the same trait Al had, the drive to gather info and solve. Al thought a lot of kids didn't seem to know how to enjoy such simple things. Take the group that went driving through the county, smashing mailboxes with baseball bats. High-school boys, probably. No joy there, just the destructive good time of breaking the possessions and property of others. Kids. Well, young thugs really in that instance.

"Want a walk, Tanner?" Al gave a gentle tug on the leash.

Tanner hesitated, wanting to follow the scent of what had taken him there. Then he broke into his brisk high-stepping trot and pulled up until he was beside but not ahead of Al.

They followed the ruts all the way to a two-lane asphalt road. A quarter of a mile down the road sat a yellow wooden house with a back wooden deck that hung out over a hill that dropped behind the house. *Must be a good view.* Al figured it was the house that went with the land all the way to the fence, but he doubted the residents looked in the direction of the shelter much.

He and Tanner started down the road, on the left side so they could watch for cars. Tanner found a few interesting things at which to sniff but with none of the intensity he'd shown when on the trail of the scent.

Al heard a growing noise as they neared the house. As they crested a hill, he saw an older man in a wide-brimmed slouch hat sitting on a Bobcat that was pushing at a stand of prickly-pear cactus. He backed away from the half-tumbled stand of cactus, its shallow roots sticking into

44

the air on one side, drove over to the fence, and turned off the motor.

In the quietness, Al and Tanner crossed the road to stand by the barbed-wire fence.

"Hell of a day for hiking about," the man said, leaning his head out of the cab, his face half in shadow from his wide-brimmed hat. "It's gonna get hotter than the ass end of hell 'fore the day's over. Haley Lamont. You can call me ol' Hale." His ears had grown large, like a small elephant's, beneath his salt-and-pepper hair, which was mostly salt. His skin on his face and arms had tanned until it was the brown of an old saddle.

Al took out his wallet and flashed his badge. "Al Quinn. You ever see anyone drive along the far side of your property late at night?"

"Nope. And if I did, they'd be carrying a load of salt rock in their britches. I've had the double-barrel loaded that way ever since those blasted kids smashed my mailbox. You guys ever do anything about them?"

"Working on it," Al lied.

"Yeah. That's what I figured." Lamont's mouth twisted on one side into a wry, knowing smile. His was a wise old country face that had been told a lot of things and come to believe very few of them, and Al had seen the expression often enough before. "Tell you what, though," the man added, "I had a guy make me a shell for the mailbox out of half-inch steel. Only a week or two later, I saw where they'd driven by and tried to knock it again. Someone broke their Louisville slugger all to ash toothpicks they left behind." He made a sound in his throat Al took to be a chuckle. His face twisted into what Al took for a wink.

"But you saw nobody over there along that fence. Right?" Al waved toward the fence-line road he and Tanner had just taken.

"Well, truth be told, I take out my hearing aid at night. The clap of doom could happen out here, and I wouldn't hear it. But I tell you, if I'd seen anyone, I'd show you what's left of them if I'd seen 'em real good."

"Okay. Thanks."

Al and Tanner turned to go back, and Lamont fired up his Bobcat and steered it back toward the half-finished job. Al could see about a hundred more stands of cactus just as big, so Mr. Lamont probably had a pretty busy summer ahead of him.

Al, Clarence, and the few crime-scene people who'd stayed to work the back-road access to the pet-rescue property were just wrapping up and heading back across the field to the buildings when Sheriff Clayton's cruiser pulled up in the shelter's parking lot.

Clayton got out of the passenger door and waved to Al. "You get anything?"

Deputy Camilla "Cam" Callaghan, in uniform, got out of the driver's-side door and put on her white department cowboy hat. She tipped the front bill toward Al with her finger and thumb.

She was tall, about five nine, but after being around six-foot-two Fergie, Al didn't find that daunting. Her face was darkly tanned, and she moved with the muscled grace of someone who spent a great deal of her free time at the gym and preferred to be there. Al caught himself sucking in his stomach then relaxed with a long outward breath. Her dirty-blond hair was cut fairly short, not enough to be radical but enough to be efficient. She was in her later thirties and had a few lines on her face, though Al didn't think they came from smiling too much. He knew she could be capable, too. She'd hung onto the windshield wiper of a guy who tried to run her over once, and she'd stayed on his car until the first sharp turn. But she'd tracked him down to the house of the guy's mistress later and had clapped on the cuffs herself.

Fit and buff though she was, next to Sheriff Clayton, she looked almost petite, as well as cheerful. Clayton was John Wayne tall, with at least as big a presence. Al had referred to Clayton too often as someone who looked like a hibernating bear who had just been prematurely roused.

"Some fresh tire tracks and a few bootprints," Al said. "Clarence will take it all in for processing."

"Mean anything to you?"

"Not yet, but it's more than we had. I'm just glad Tanner here didn't lead us to a beef jerky wrapper out there or something. He picked up a scent by the incinerator and took us right out there. I think it's a good connection. We'll see."

"Only two other shelters on the list are out from town, have incinerators, and have roads that might allow a back way in. We'll seal them until the crews can rest and work them tomorrow. Good enough for you?" Clayton said.

"Yeah, these guys need a break."

"Where'd you get the pint-sized bloodhound?"

"He's new to my household. I just happened to have him along. Good thing I did."

"Well, you can pick up on the trail again tomorrow. I'd like Cam here to ride along with you. She can come pick you up. That okay with you?"

"Sure."

"You can leave that behind." Cam pointed down at Tanner. She had a terse, clipped way of talking, a regular Joe Friday type, from the old *Dragnet* show, as if each word cost her money or pain.

"He's not part of my usual come-along. Why? Don't you like dogs?"

"A dog bit me once." That was all she said. She looked away toward the shelter, where some barking and stirring was going on.

Al wondered what other things had happened to her once. She could be brusque and even a touch surly. Maybe some guy had bitten her once, too. He had a notion if her choice of partners was left up to her, she'd rather not have a man like him along, either.

CHAPTER FIVE

A L STOOD OUTSIDE HIS FRONT door at a quarter to eight the next morning. He felt off balance, alone, as if he'd left one of his legs behind. Tanner had been eager to come along until Fergie and Bonnie had smothered him with petting and then put him on his leash for a walk out the back side of the house to the lake. Even then, Tanner had looked back over his shoulder at Al a couple of times as he was being led away. Al didn't know how much he was reading into Tanner's looks, but he thought the dog looked a little hurt, let down. *"I thought we were going to be together, always"*—that sort of thing.

The wind swayed the upper limbs of the trees back and forth in the gusting wind. Al concentrated on those branches the way he did on his own breathing when he was having trouble falling asleep. Funny. When he could look down and see Tanner curled up and sleeping like a faithful guard beside the bed, he hadn't had any trouble dozing off himself.

Tanner might well benefit from being away from Al's constant presence. They were both adjusting to new circumstances and maybe needed space now and then— good for them both. He kept telling himself that until the cruiser pulled up his lane and swung in front. He opened the door and got in. Cam kept both hands on the wheel and barely glanced his way. Al's former partner used to have a cup of coffee waiting for him. No such luck with Cam.

"I left the dog behind today," he said as she pulled away.

"Good."

She reminded him of the way people spoke in Maine. He'd gone land-locked salmon fishing up there years before, and after a Texas summer of blowtorch heat, the coolness had felt delicious. He asked a local who sat outside a bait-and-tackle shop if he'd lived here long.

"Thirty year," the man said. His squinting blue eyes peered out from beneath two tangled white-and-gray caterpillars of eyebrows.

"Do you like it here?"

"Yep."

"Anything you don't like about it?" Al asked, thinking of the bitterly cold winters.

"Well," the man had said, "six months a year, it's hotter'n the devil up here."

Al thought of that fellow, windy by comparison with Cam, as they headed toward the first shelter.

"I'd like to talk to this fellow Jeff at the first rescue-dog shelter. Then we can pop in on the other spots to see if the crews are turning up anything there."

"You don't seem very cheerful," she said with no hint of a smile.

"Well, I just heard a high-school classmate of mine died. That's the third to go from that class this year. Then, right on top of that, I heard that my old college roommate kicked off. That one rattled me even more. I've been trying to figure out why I care about a college roommate who died. We hadn't even stayed close, didn't have that much in common."

"I'd heard you're kind of soft."

"How's that being soft?" He looked toward her.

She didn't glance his way, instead staying fixed on the road ahead. "Well, he's your age, isn't he? You're probably just sweating your own mortality."

After that, the ride was one long silence.

———◆———

While they were still college roommates, Kevin Beale had surged into their two-bedroom apartment one night at close to two in the morning, flinging the door open and grinning widely, his curly light-brown hair bouncing. Always full of surprises, he'd said he was headed down to the corner for a six-pack, but his hands were empty. Two girls came in the door behind him, both looking around at the apartment and at Al, who was sitting in just his boxer shorts at their small dinette table, using it as a desk.

"Hey, look what I found," Kevin shouted. "They said they wanted to party."

A black girl in jeans with holes at the knees stayed close to Kevin. A skinny redhead was staring at Al. He supposed he'd been promised to her from the way she fixed on him.

"You guys go ahead and party without me," Al said.

"I don't mind," the redhead said. She tilted her head and fiddled with her long, straight hair, pulling it behind one shell-pink ear on one side.

Al didn't say it, but he thought, *Well, I do.* He shook his head.

He saw the rejection move across her face and suspected she'd felt that sort of sting before, often enough. Maybe that was even what drove her to casual sex with people like Kevin. He felt bad for a moment, sorry he'd hurt her without meaning to. Then she flipped him off and spun on the heel of her Converse All-Star sneaker, giving him a farewell scowl as she and the other girl followed Kevin toward his room. Al felt better then. But only a little.

After they'd all clumped into Kevin's room and closed the door behind them, Al thought about the girl, someone's daughter or sister. That moment defined the essential difference between him and Kevin, something that kept them from being any closer than they were. However, he'd felt something pluck at him deep inside when he'd heard Kevin was gone.

That had been just one incident in a litany of many in Kevin's college carousing, one Al never looked back on as a missed opportunity. He had sometimes credited that moment with stirring whatever had made him get serious about Abbie, enough that they lived together the next year while Kevin got a new roommate, one even wilder than himself. Al found it hard to believe Kevin, once so full of vitality, was dead. He was just one of many friends who had drifted away over the years and whom Al had not kept up with the way he might have.

Kevin had not been that abnormal of a college student, one chasing more than grades. He called Al "a stodgy, stuffy stick-in-the mud." Al realized for the first time how rigid his own moral compass could be. He'd tried not to be judgmental about others, though that had been a stretch with the business between Maury and Abbie. Still, it might have been what sent him into law enforcement as a career.

Through the years, he'd been the one to loosen up while putting in his years at the sheriff's department. Some of the rising young Turks he found a little stiff recently, like the ramrod beside him still clutching the steering wheel, hands so tight in the ten-and-two position that her knuckles were going a little white.

A Lincoln Town Car ahead of them with two aged and fading McCain/Palin bumper stickers weaved to the left of the yellow stripe a couple of times. Wrong time of day for the driver to be half in the bag, so Al suspected a cell phone of causing the distraction.

Al might have kidded that anyone that Republican ought to find it easy to stay on the right side of the road. He glanced her way, caught her stern look, and said nothing—not a good time for joking. He waited to see what she'd do. But Cam didn't light up the car and pull it over. She ignored it. They were almost to their destination, and she stayed true to her purpose.

Al realized he was staring out the window ahead and to the side, the same way his dog had, until they pulled in to the shelter where he'd gotten Tanner.

He reached for his door handle.

"Wait a minute," she said.

He turned toward her.

"Let me understand your status. You're not a real deputy, just a temporary advisor, and you're not a superior with advisory powers but just a kind of *ad hoc* consultant. Right?"

"Except for one thing."

"What's that?"

"Clayton believes me and trusts me. He's gonna want to know if you're worthy of promoting. My opinion draws water." He opened his door and got out, giving her time to stew on that.

He was struggling to be open-minded and fair. He'd always thought Cam too "by the book." She could be prim, neat, curt, and all for procedure and rules when sometimes a deputy has to think faster than those allow. Still, her record was good, and he couldn't deny that she was bright. But she'd gone out of her way to clip his wings, and he liked his wings right where they were.

They walked to the front of the shelter in silence. He caught her glancing his way from time to time, peeking at him from under the brim of her hat.

Myra Henningdale stood just outside the front door, waiting on them. She looked pensive or tired, maybe a bit of both. Still, she reached up, touched her temple with two fingers and managed a weak smile for Al and a raised eyebrow for Cam.

"This is Deputy Callaghan," Al said. "We'd like to chat with Jeff if we could—then Megan if she's around."

"It's why I'm waiting out here. Jeff's with the dogs, and Megan... She's with him, but well, she needed a few moments to compose herself. This has been stressful on us all."

"We understand," Al said.

Cam darted him a quick look that said, *"The hell we do."*

Myra led the way through the cages, and the dogs gave them the sort of clamor Cam would get if she were a woman walking through a men's prison. As the dogs barked, a few even growling and snapping, Al felt Cam move closer until she was between Myra and Al.

"They're mostly noise and enthusiasm," Al said. "They don't mean you any harm."

"That's right. A few might lick you to death, but once they're out of their cages, most of them are real teddy bears," Myra said.

"Look." Al glanced toward Myra then eased close to a cage where an orange-and-white low, squat dog that looked half bulldog and half pit bull pressed against its cage, barking.

Myra nodded.

Al held his hand out, and the dog's tongue shot outside to lick his hand. He put his fingers inside the cage, and the dog licked at him as if he were candy, its eyes fixed on him all the while. As he took his hand out, the dog's tail wagged in frantic rhythm, and it let out a low whine. Cam was staring at Al as if he'd just put his head in a lion's mouth.

"You wouldn't want to try that with just any strange dog, but Myra knows that all that dog wants is someone to love," Al said.

Myra was wearing a twisted welcome-to-my-world smile.

They found Jeff at a grooming table, trimming the toenails of a black-with-brown-ears dachshund. Megan, wearing thick gloves, was helping. That was two birds with one stone, as Al saw it. Cam looked as though she would prefer to separate them for any grilling, but she deferred. Megan looked up at them first, with an almost perfectly round face above a body that wasn't far behind in being as round. She had red curly hair and an impish grin, and her skin was so pale her thick sprays of freckles stood out like constellations.

Al glanced around the room. A set of white shelves held the bare minimum of pet medicines and supplies. He also saw a sink, the table, and a couple of what looked like support harnesses for them to use while working on animals—he wasn't sure. The place was a shoestring operation, that was for sure, but he doubted they would supplement the budget by doing cremations. If they did, then they probably wouldn't have reported finding the human bones. That quick loop of thought played itself out.

"Sadie's a bit of a nipper, but only when her space is violated." Jeff looked up at them through oversized tortoise-shell glasses. His hair was short and dark and his face mottled with the scars of what had probably been a rough bout of acne as a teen. He looked serious one second, yet a waiting smile lurked like the sun about to come from behind a cloud. "She's fine with kids. Toenails are tricky. With dark nails, it's hard to tell where the quick is. You wouldn't want to try this at home. There. That's the last one."

Sadie, who had a jaw grip on Megan's gloved thumb, let go and turned to Jeff. He patted her head, then Megan lifted Sadie down to put her in a small travel cage, what Al had seen called training crates at the pet store. She was wagging her little stubby tail and looking at Megan with such happy joy. Hard to believe she'd had her jaws clamped on Megan's thumb just seconds before.

"You're a good dog, Sadie," Megan said. "We won't have to do that again for a while, maybe never if someone takes you home. You're a cutie."

Cam's eyes had opened wider and stayed fixed like laser beams on the glove Megan had worn while Sadie was biting her thumb.

"What is it, Cam?" Al said.

She shook herself. "Did you know that nearly six thousand mail carriers were bitten by dogs last year? Figures just came out. Houston was the number-one city in America for incidents."

"And that's germane to what? You're not a mail carrier."

Cam looked at him, though not in full focus. Something was playing far back in her head—a bad movie, from the twist of her mouth. He noticed for the first time that she had brown eyes. *Kind of odd for a blond. Not like me to have missed that before.*

"Let's get this over with," she said.

Jeff moved over to a sink, turned the water on, and

washed his hands. Al had noticed the young man's hands were reddish and chapped. He probably washed them hundreds of times a day—just a tidbit of info to store away.

"Not all of this job must be fun." Al eased closer. "Do you mind doing some of the grooming too in a small, lightly-staffed place like this?"

"Not really. I worked summers in a pet store, got plenty of that sort of thing."

Before Al could ask one or two more establishing-rapport questions, Cam stepped closer. "Do you have any idea how human bones got in the incinerator? Did you see anyone do it? Do you know who might have?"

"No. No. And no." He turned to Cam. Anything like a smile had washed from his face. His eyes tightened as his eyes went back and forth between them. Al could sense the deflector shields going up and tightening into place.

"We said everything in the statements we wrote out," Megan said. "Haven't you found anything like a clue that could tell us who is doing this? It's creepy thinking of someone coming onto the property and doing 'we don't know what' and us not even knowing they were coming and going."

Al turned to her and smiled. "I know you're both tired and have thought about this a lot. You don't know anything that would help us, do you?"

She shook her head, and he turned to Jeff, who did the same.

"Thanks for your help," Al said. "Let's go, Cam."

"But I..."

He was already walking.

Cam caught up with him in the hallway. "Look, I know you don't like me, but—"

"We'll talk in the car," Al said.

Her mouth clamped tight, and she beat him to the car.

As they passed Myra, who stood in the hallway outside her office, she caught whatever expression was wrestling on Cam's face and didn't say anything. Al gave her a low wave, which she returned with a wink thrown in.

Cam slammed her door, and Al got in and closed his side with exaggerated quiet. He turned toward her. Steam wasn't coming out of her ears, but he wouldn't have been surprised if it had been.

"Look, you might be asshole buddies with Sheriff Clayton," she said, "but I don't intend to let some good-old-boy network get in the way of me and my goals."

He started to speak then stopped himself, to take time to play back everything she'd said that day, something he'd seen Clayton do often.

Al decided not to critique her interviewing and interrogation skills. He let her stew in her own juices to get it on her own. The lesson would stick better if she came to the discovery and insight herself. His respect for how Clayton handled the department grew.

"You might as well understand something," she said. "This is an opportunity for me. Clayton's had me running around all over this part of the county, looking into these petty, stupid burglaries when they're probably being done by the same bunch of punk kids who went around smashing mailboxes a while back. Their folks should have been stricter, maybe even drowned a few of them when they were young."

Al leaned back in his seat, more than amazed at the cornucopia of words pouring from her, which had to be cathartic for her. He let her vent.

She sat with both hands on the wheel, ten-and-two position, eyes forward, though she hadn't started the engine yet. "You might as well know I intend to be sheriff here someday. In this county. My goal is nothing less than that. Sheriff Clayton is such a, such a..."

Al waited. *This will be a good one.*

"A thing of the past. He wants to do everything according to some code that went out with King Arthur, as far as I'm concerned. Do you know about the Hispanics—the *Latinos*, I should say these days?" Her head turned toward him, eyes fixed on his.

When he said nothing, she said, "He wants us to consider their crimes and those we stop on a case-by-case basis, when ICE would prefer to just get them all handed over and then deported. I've crunched the numbers. We could be sending three times the number we do back to Mexico, and ICE could be doing all the heavy lifting. Less work and bother for the department and more time to handle the overload of work we have."

"You mean deport even the ones who haven't done major crimes?"

"Yeah. Why not?"

"You find nothing biased or prejudiced in that?"

"To hell with all that PC crap. A lot would be cleared off our blotters, and I mean right now."

Her voice had risen in the car. Al was thinking back with fondness to the time he could barely get a word out of her. She was taking deep breaths, getting back in control. He watched her eyes and guessed she was playing back much of what she'd just said, checking to see if she'd said too much.

"Is that about the whole load?" he said. "Is that what is really bugging you?"

"No." Her voice quivered for the first time. "I just don't understand."

He waited. "What is it you don't understand?"

"Look, we have a huge department, over three hundred deputies, three times that in corrections, with captains, majors, and a chief deputy. We have five detective spots.

Why does the sheriff take a personal interest in some things and keep someone like you on to watch me when you should stay retired? Why does he keep a flinty old piece of rope like you around and not just let you retire like others have done? Let the young bucks and other detectives on the force rise and do their jobs."

"I don't know," Al said, his voice a lot calmer than hers. "I've wondered a bit myself. Maybe I'm a good-luck piece or like an old pair of boots, worn and comfortable—not pretty, but I do get the job done."

"Not always along the most orthodox path if I've heard right."

"Do you think you'll run a much tighter ship when you're sheriff?"

She sat frozen in place, her eyes darting left then right.

Al's first thought was that she had said a lot, maybe too much, far too much. *She has to know that.*

"Maybe we should go look at the other sites now," he said.

"Yes, we could do that." Stiff as an unoiled robot, she turned forward and started the car.

Al's phone rang. He held up a hand and dug for his phone with the other. "Hold on a moment."

CHAPTER SIX

A L BARELY GOT IN A hello then listened for over a minute before he closed his cell phone. Cam watched him, her eyes narrowed, brow furrowed.

"That was Clive," he said. "We've got one more, but that's it. The other sites were clean."

"Where to?" she asked.

"Other side of town. Looks like whoever's behind this was spreading things out. This place is off Anderson Mill Road. Clive's still at the site."

She shifted into drive and opened up the squad car, letting the big Interceptor motor roar as they peeled out of the drive, slid a foot or two in the gravel, and shot off down the highway.

It seemed to please her to be driving and driving fast, going somewhere. Her face nearly broke into a smile, but he watched her get the best of showing anything like real emotion as she wrestled her face back into stony determination. He saw her catch herself leaning forward and, in response, press her shoulders back against her seat.

Al took in her uniform. Most detectives could wear plain clothes, but she'd elected to wear her uniform, perhaps thinking it commanded more respect and got better cooperation. Not a single wrinkle. She sure used plenty of starch.

Back when he'd started at the department so long

before, he'd found two types of fellow law officers to steer clear of and avoid as a partner. Those were the heavy badges and the gun-leaners. The gun-leaners were the cocky, confident officers, some of whom, as often as not, had gotten their starts giving other kids wedgies out on the playground. The heavy badges were often authority conscious to a fault. Al would have numbered Cam among the heavy badges if he hadn't long ago given up that sort of evaluation, which was as prone to error as any sort of labeling.

"What happened with all those burglaries you were looking into?" he asked.

"What?" She gave him a quick glance.

"Did you solve them?"

"No. But I have a darn good hunch who was doing it."

"Who?"

"Some of the same kids who'd driven around smashing mailboxes."

"How'd you figure that?"

"Found an aluminum bat they'd used to break into one place. No prints, but it was missing from a school's bat bag. The school, Del Valley High School, kept a record. They also have the team manager stamp the school initials in the butt end."

"So it was students."

"I wish." She frowned at him. "The coach and I talked to every student on the team. I doubt there's enough larceny among them to steal a base. Fine kids, though. They said they didn't do it, and I believed them as well as the coach. Outrageous waste of my time. Then the coach remembered he had the team van serviced at a local garage."

"What'd you find there?" Al kept her talking since she was easier to be with when going over the details of a case.

"It's what I didn't find. Guy named Toby Buchanan

had worked there, was out with a broken arm. The owner found that several tools had taken a hike, and he'd told Toby not to come back."

"I know Toby. Lanky fellow. Some of the worst teeth I've ever seen. They've eroded in the middle, like each tooth has a waist, and that part is either green or black."

Cam snapped a glance Al's way.

"He has a sheet too, a few priors that fit."

"Right. I know that." She stared ahead again. "It was enough to get a warrant, but his place was clean. Not a single burgled item showed up at his place."

"But you think it was him behind some of the burglaries and the smashed mailboxes as well."

"I know damn well it was. But I have squat. And I have to walk soft now, or he's apt to lawyer up and start squealing 'harassment' or some such crap."

"What about his partner?"

"What partner?"

"He had to have at least one, someone to drive the truck or car. Probably a friend—could even work at the same garage."

"Oh, crap."

"What?"

"I missed that. I shouldn't have." She hesitated. "You think I'm a lousy detective, right?"

"I think you're kind of hard on yourself when you don't need to be."

They went back into quiet mode for the rest of the ride. He could have told her he had a hunch how Toby might've broken his arm. He thought back to Haley Lamont's place and how the man had put a steel shell around his mailbox and had found a splintered bat the next morning. Hitting something like that from a car passing at speed might well break more than the bat. But he kept that to himself for the moment.

She pulled into a driveway not long after passing a series of entrances to a gravel pit or quarry with enormous trucks lumbering in and out of each entrance.

A roadrunner trotted across the road in front of them from right to left. Al was glad it was stepping lively because Cam didn't slow for it.

"I always think it's good luck when I see a roadrunner," he said.

She let air out of her nose in a derisive snort without looking at him. Before working with her, he'd often wondered why she never seemed to be in a relationship. But he was getting clues.

"You know, I have a hunch how Toby might've gotten his broken arm. It has to do with the mailbox vandalism. We wrap up this business with the bones, and I'll see what I can do to help you with Toby."

"You don't have to do me any favors," she said.

He looked at her.

"I mean I'd like to solve it on my own. If you don't mind." Her mouth settled into a firm, pinched line.

High on the ridge of the limestone that rose off to one side of the pet shelter, a man lowered his binoculars. With his left arm, he let the limb of mountain laurel ease back into place. He spoke into a Jawbone Bluetooth headset, one equipped with military-grade NoiseAssassin and wind-canceling technology, the kind originally developed for use by tank commanders and helicopter pilots to eliminate background noise. "There are cops swarming this place too. It's out, same as the others. I've got to do something. The car's beginning to smell."

"Use your ingenuity."

"Landfill?"

"No need to tell me. Just make it clean... and permanent this time." The voice abruptly clicked off.

The man rose and headed toward a silver Dodge minivan. He'd cracked the windows, but that wasn't helping much. He glanced at his watch, calculating the time until darkness would fall. *The landfill. Easy for him to say. Damned place has a fence now, too. Everything was so much easier before.*

———◆———

Cam pulled her cruiser up behind Clive's Volvo, which was parked as close as he could get it to the yellow tape running along a row of stakes around the incinerator.

"They checked four other places," Al said. "Clayton tells me this is the only one where they also found human bones. The other places were either locked up better or didn't have back roads that let anyone come in from a different direction."

She grabbed her hat from the ring that held it upside down above the inside top of the windshield, opened her door, and got out, not saying a word.

"Gonna be a long day," Al muttered to himself.

He got out of the passenger side just as Clarence waved and climbed into the crime-scene van.

Clive had the back of his Volvo open, and Teddy was coming toward him with a shovel and a rack.

"There you are," Clive said. "Glad you could make it. We're just wrapping up and going to head back to the lab. But you were right, Al. Three out of seven possible places all seem to be body-dump sites."

When Clive held out a hand, Al shook it and waved toward Cam. "You know Detective Callaghan, don't you?"

"Sure." Clive held out his hand to her.

Cam walked past him and looked inside the back of the Volvo. Teddy had to step out of the way. She gave Al half a grin but didn't look at Cam. Al could tell Teddy was tired, running on borrowed gas. The last few days probably had been too full of people for her taste. She could easily get crowded socially, and when she did, her eye contact with others suffered. Al imagined she was eager to get back to the lab, where her work with Clive would be less public.

"Where are the bones?" Cam turned to look at Clive.

"Back at the lab," he said. "We're just wrapping up and on our way to join them."

"What have you found so far?"

Clive glanced toward Al then panned back to Cam. "It's too early to know as much as we'd like. We got human remains from three animal-shelter incinerators. The others were okay. We've asked the city to check theirs, but so far nada there."

"And the bones?"

"All younger women. In their early – to midthirties."

"Hmm. Ethnicity?"

"Asian. At least, I think so, if the scrap of skull we got is any indication."

"Oh. I was expecting Latino," Cam said. "Do you think human trafficking?"

"I don't think anything yet. I follow the evidence alone. It's up to folks like you and Al to make something of it, to hypothesize if need be."

"Well, it's kind of obvious, isn't it?" Cam said.

"Nothing's obvious to me. I'm a scientist. I'm always open to where the evidence leads. I try not to get ahead of it."

Cam frowned at him.

Al figured she thought Clive was taking a shot at her

with that, but that had been Clive's stance for years. He refused to speculate. Ever.

Clarence closed the back doors on the crime-scene lab van and waved at Al. He came over to them.

"Where's your little pooch? We could have used him," Clarence said.

"He's at home today."

"Too bad. But I did borrow your idea and had a K-9 unit come by and help today. No luck, though. I think our second site is the freshest."

"You get anything from the tire tracks at the second place?" Al asked.

"Dodge minivan. That narrows it right down to just a few thousand possibilities."

"It's a start," Al said.

Cam let out a snort, turned, and almost ran into Teddy, who was carrying an empty tray and sifter, the last of Clive's gear, to the Volvo. Teddy flinched the way someone would when expecting to get hit, and she kept her eyes averted. Al could tell the girl had worked like a trouper and was probably as tired as she could be, but she'd never complained once.

Cam curled a lip but said nothing, at least until she and Al were back in the car.

"You know, they ought to let that girl go."

"Teddy? Why?"

"She's retarded or something."

"She's not retarded. She has a touch of autism. Clive says she's the best assistant he's ever had."

"Then he's half the idiot she is, and she's an idiot big time."

Al felt blasts of heat brightening his cheeks and had to fight to keep his hands flat on his legs and not let them curl into fists. He had used his flashes of anger in the past in combative moments. He'd hurt some men and killed a few others. He didn't care much for the way using the barely channeled rage made him feel later, but doing so had kept him alive once or twice.

When he was a hair calmer, he said, "That's not a very politically correct or sensitive thing to say."

"Hey, I don't care if I make everyone happy. Being sheriff isn't about winning a popularity contest."

"Actually, it kind of is. You have to win a public election." He had nearly reminded her of how a decision is made for advancement. He suddenly realized she didn't intend to go up the ladder but wanted to shoot straight for the top.

Her mouth tightened, and she glared at the road ahead and turned as chatty as a snail with laryngitis the rest of the way to his house, which was fine with him.

At the house, she pulled up and stopped but kept her face straight ahead, not saying a word.

"Hey, I'm sorry," she said as he reached for the door handle.

"About what?" He turned back to her.

"About calling that girl a retard. She might well be, but it's not my place to point it out."

Al nodded and managed a quick smile. He'd have to think about that. *Had Cam just been genuinely apologetic, or just covering her can?*

Al got out his door and closed it, and she was off in a short spray of gravel.

He heard Tanner barking just inside the door but paused, took out his cell phone, and punched in a familiar number.

Sheriff Clayton answered, "What's up?"

"I was wondering if you had anything particular in mind with this arrangement?"

"I figure you'll figure it out. It's best that way."

"Any tips or suggestions?"

"Nope. You're on your own. You're a detective. See what you can detect."

Clayton hung up, and Al put his cell phone away. The moment he swung the door open, Tanner leaped out at him with the most enthusiasm Al had seen from him yet. His paws were on Al's leg, and he licked at Al's hand as if he were holding a fistful of treats.

"I believe he missed you." Maury was sitting on the couch, and he put a bookmark in the book he held, closed it, and put it on the coffee table. "He's been by the front door most of the day. Wouldn't budge even when I wanted to put a webcam on him and have him follow the gals into their showers."

Bonnie stuck her head around the corner. "Good. You're just in time. Dinner's on. Thought we'd have fun with your pooch today, but he mostly sat and stared at the door."

The house seemed darker than usual for that time of day. The lights from the dining area flickered the way candles do.

As his eyes adjusted to the light, Al could make out that Maury was wearing a white shirt and pressed khaki pants and was reaching up to tighten the knot of a red-and-blue tie into place. When he saw Al observing his clothes, he held up the flat of a hand, made the sign of zipping his lip, and waved Al closer. Maury stood up and leaned forward. Tanner moved closer to Al's leg, his nose sniffing in high gear.

"Just a word of warning," Maury whispered. "It's dress-up night. I think the natives are restless and want a sacrifice. Since they mostly ignore me altogether, I suspect it's you. Checked the moon schedule. Tonight's almost a full moon. Thought I'd let you know. Imagine that! We have to dress up just to eat."

"Where'd you get the shirt? And I know that's my tie."

The white dress shirt hung off Maury's narrow shoulders. "Don't worry. There are plenty more white shirts in your closet," Maury said.

"What do you mean *sacrifice*?"

"I don't know. My vision is you tied naked to a rock and one or both of them doing all sorts of things to you—naked things, illegal in some states."

"I think you just have too much time on your hands. Your imagination's getting the best of you."

Al eased around Maury and went through the dining area. The table was set with his best dishes, wine glasses, and flatware. Two tall white tapers were lit in holders. Both Fergie and Bonnie wore what looked like backless gowns beneath their aprons. Fergie's dress was black. Bonnie wore red. They turned and grinned, waving at him in near unison. Maury had been right. The women were up to something. He could imagine covens with less sinister smiles.

He headed to his bedroom and felt safer there for the moment. Tanner shot forward and squeezed in after him just as he closed the door.

"Are they giving you a case of the willies too?" Al asked.

Tanner stretched out flat on the floor with his paws out in front and his head resting on them while he watched Al dig through his closet, find some clothes he considered business casual, and switch into them.

"Dressing for dinner. Humpf." He knew women sometimes wanted to dress nicely, dine out, and maybe even dance a few numbers.

Abbie had taught him that. "Women's needs are different from men's," she'd said.

In fairness, she hadn't cared for fishing. She had liked dining and dancing. His time hadn't been such to do much of that dining and dancing sort of thing lately, and he certainly wouldn't have thought of it while living alone.

He opened the door and caught the sound of Max Bruch's *Violin Concerto Number One in G Minor* playing on the stereo, the Ruggerio Ricci version, his favorite. He'd once said it was the most romantic piece in all classical music. He immediately tried to remember to whom he'd said that.

The lights were dimmer, and someone had started a fire in the fireplace even though they'd had to turn up the air conditioning to pull that off. Maury sat at the table, the candle lights flickering in his wide eyes saying, "Run, Al, run!"

Al sat down across the table from Maury. He spotted no name tags, thank heaven, but he figured they would be chatting so the women and men should alternate. Wine was in the glass beside his plate. He took a sip. *Quite good.* That didn't make him feel any calmer.

"The salad is one you said you liked." Bonnie put the small bowls beside each plate. "Endive and thin purple onions with red-wine vinegar and olive oil." She had her apron off, and her red dress dipped low enough in front for what was in her lift-and-push bra to nearly win the battle it was fighting.

Fergie brought the entrée to the table, and Al had to admit her long red flowing hair looked terrific by candlelight. "Another favorite of yours. Monkfish—and done as the 'poor man's lobster' the way you like, with drawn butter." Her black dress wasn't as daring as Bonnie's, but she flowed beneath it like one of the sirens from the sea. Al glanced toward Maury, whose eyes had gotten wider.

The music, the wine, and the food soon relaxed Al.

Though all through dinner, Tanner stayed right by Al's feet, looking up at him.

"I think you're supposed to drop him a tidbit now and then," Fergie said.

"Lady at the pet-food store said he'll do better if he stays with his regular food and treats. People food might upset his stomach. But we can find a more elevating subject than that. Anything new with you two?" He glanced from Fergie to Bonnie and back to Fergie again, catching them exchanging a quick glance.

"Well, Fergie's being pursued for a PI position with another retired Austin cop, Douglas Chandle. Do you know him?" Bonnie asked.

"Oh, I know him." Al turned to Fergie. "Isn't that a lot of domestic stuff? Cheating husbands and vice versa?"

"If that was all he did, I wouldn't even be considering it. But he does some industrial and insurance investigation work too—says he has a big fish on the line. That sounds more interesting and up my alley. Besides, it's something to keep me busy, and I can't keep living off what I got for my house being burned down." Fergie lifted a forkful of monkfish to her mouth. A drop of butter fell from it and ran down from the corner of her full lips—sensual.

Al looked away then toward Maury and back toward Bonnie. Her mouth was twisted into an impish smile.

"Well, then, that's okay with me, if you're asking. I have no issue with you getting a job. Is that what this soiree was all about, a celebration for that?" He went for his last bite of monkfish.

"No. Can't a couple ladies just dress up once in a blue moon because they'd like to be treated right now and again?" Bonnie grinned.

"If I'd known in advance, I'd have brought flowers." Al chuckled, thinking he'd made a small joke.

"You should have." Bonnie didn't grin that time.

Al glanced at Maury, who stared back with baleful eyes that said the subtext of the moment was pretty much on the table now. Storm clouds continued to gather in the corners of the room.

What the hell? Al caught himself squirming in his seat. He and Maury must seem a couple of clumsy and inexperienced bachelors. Al could be tough and Maury smooth, but they were both downright twitchy at the moment just because they'd been asked to dress for dinner. He glanced down toward Tanner, who had his head on his outstretched paws and was looking up at Al.

"I think getting a dog was a smart thing for you, Al. It'll help ease you out of your shell." Bonnie said, shifting the subject to a far more comfortable one.

She bent over to pet Tanner, the top of her dress dipping open, and Maury didn't even ogle as usual. Instead, Maury's stare stayed fixed on Al, his eyes getting bigger, as if Al were about to be pitched into a pot by cannibals.

Bonnie sat back upright. "A lot of people get pets when raw affection isn't readily available in their lives."

"You know, I suspect someone very dear to that dog was taken away or went away, and Tanner's biggest fear is that it might happen again." Fergie was dabbing at her lips with a napkin.

"Anything special in mind tonight?" Al asked. *Might as well face the music.*

"We just wanted a night where we could enjoy each other, think about how it could be the next few years," Bonnie said, her voice dripping with innocence.

"How what could be?" Al said.

"Oh, don't try to play dense. No one's ever going to ascribe that to you," Fergie said. "All we're saying is we could have some more elegant times together instead of getting into any quotidian rut. It's just nice for a change. Don't you think?"

"Sure," Al said. "Sure. Sure."

He glanced toward Maury, who looked just about ready to leap out of his chair and run, and not just because Fergie had used the word *quotidian* instead of saying "everyday humdrum." Maury had spent a lifetime moving quickly so he wouldn't end up with a ring in his nose, and since he fancied himself a "player," that had meant more than a few peaks and valleys to his pursuit of happiness.

That seemed to mark the end of the threatening storm clouds in the room. Fergie began to talk about the new job, how it would be nice to be active again. The tension slowly eased from the room, they finished the last of the wine, and Bonnie and Fergie shooed Al from the room.

"Get your rest," Bonnie said.

Maury saw his chance and headed to Al's bathroom to change into his pajamas. When Al finished his after-dinner coffee and left the table, Tanner stayed right at his heels.

Maury dumped Al's clothes on his dresser. "Whew, I'm glad that conversation went no further than it did."

"You know, for a ladies' man, you were pretty nervous about nothing." Al kicked off his burgundy loafers and started undoing his shirt.

"Oh, that was no kind of nothing, Al. That was very much about something. I don't know why my shorts got in a bunch, though. All that had nothing to do with me."

"You think I'm the bull's-eye on their dartboard?"

Maury nodded, his Adam's apple shifting in jerks along his neck.

For a moment, Al had been relaxing. However, some of the earlier tension still hung in the air. Maury gave a quick, nervous wave, left Al's room, and closed the door behind him. Al considered locking the door for a moment.

Al had a lot to think about, but that had been their point, he guessed. Al stripped and got into the shower, and Tanner came in, too.

"Well, I guess you could use a shower, too," Al said.

He reached down to scrub some soap into Tanner's back. He *had* been smelling more than a little like a dog. Tanner arched his back and let Al's fingers dig in. He gave Al his *"Yeah, that's the place"* look.

Al started thinking ahead to how he was going to be able to leave Tanner at the house again the next day. That didn't bode well with Tanner sticking to him like a tattoo.

With the lights out, he lay in bed. Usually, he thought over the details of the day's investigations. That night, he thought about the two ladies who lived at his house and what each wanted. Tanner snored softly. Soon, Al joined him.

CHAPTER SEVEN

A<small>L BLINKED HIS EYES OPEN</small> in the dark room, feeling his arm being pulled around a lanky nude body in front of him, her taut, muscled back pressed to him.

"Just hold me," Fergie said. "That's all I want right now."

"Tanner," Al muttered, "you're a helluva watchdog. That's all I've got to say."

"Don't lay it on him. He's the dog that didn't bark in the Sherlock Holmes story is all."

The significant detail in that story, Al knew all too well, was the dog not barking, which had told Holmes his case had been an inside job by someone the dog knew. The way he saw it, Al's bed had just been burgled, or at the least invaded.

She nestled back against him. His eyes closed, and soon he was asleep again.

He woke next what seemed seconds later, but the room was less dim, with morning light just coming in around the edges of the curtains. He felt a small, round, firm belly pressed against his back as well as a great deal of additional warm softness. Bonnie was doing the nuzzling and purring that time.

"String bean had to go to work with that PI guy," Bonnie said into his ear, her breath warm, as was every nude part of her pressed against him. "I didn't want you to catch a chill."

"Tanner?" Al asked out loud.

"He's okay." Bonnie nestled closer. "I let him out a while ago. He's back in and asleep again."

"I just hope no burglar ever comes to this house," Al said.

"Oh, I'm sure he'd be more assertive then. How about you, Al? Feeling assertive at all?"

Al lifted his wrist to glance at his watch. "Gotta get up and shower. Got another day with my swell new partner."

He climbed out of the bed, walked naked across the room into the bathroom, endured her wolf whistle, and turned on the shower. Tanner came barreling into the bathroom.

"Don't take too long in there," Bonnie called out, "or I'll start to think you're doing what I offered to do for you."

Al shook his head and stepped into the shower. Tanner shot in too and crowded close to Al's ankles.

"Hey, you don't need a shower every day."

Tanner just looked up at him until he soaped his hands and reached down to give Tanner the soapy back-arching rub he wanted.

"I probably shouldn't be nice to you after the lousy watchdog job you did."

Tanner looked up at him with eyes half-closed in pleasure, giving Al a *"just keep rubbing, and we're still aces"* look.

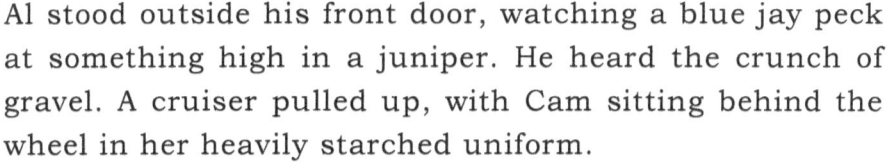

Al stood outside his front door, watching a blue jay peck at something high in a juniper. He heard the crunch of gravel. A cruiser pulled up, with Cam sitting behind the wheel in her heavily starched uniform.

"I've got someplace I'd like us to go before we get on with our other chores today," he said as he slid into the passenger seat. He gave her Haley Lamont's address.

She frowned but put the car in gear, and they were off without another word.

As they passed the rescue-dog shelter and kennel that Taylor James ran, Al saw no sign of the crime-scene crew that had traipsed all over the place. Hell, he'd traipsed with them. Ahead was Haley's place.

Al spotted Haley as they came up the road to his spread. He wasn't on his Bobcat. He'd piled all the prickly-pear cactus and scrub brush into rows that could dry and be burned later. He was riding a big green John Deere tractor between the rows, dragging a brush hog behind to mow what was left. A big cloud of dust rose behind the tractor.

Haley saw the cruiser, so he turned off the mower, raised the brush hog, and drove over to the fence. Cam pulled the cruiser onto the shoulder and stopped on the other side of the fence from where Haley sat on his tractor. She and Al got out and went over to the fence. Haley turned off the tractor so he could hear.

Al called out, "Ol' Hale. How're you doing? This is Cam. We'd like to talk."

"Well, hell. I've always got time for that. There're days I'd talk to a stump." Haley climbed off the tractor, moving slowly on what looked to Al like rheumatic knees. He took off his wide-brimmed straw hat and left it on the tractor seat. The wind tugged at his white hair, sending two thick, matted clumps of it in different directions.

When he got to the fence, he held out a hand. Al shook it. Haley's hand looked like a big-knuckled catcher's mitt and felt like leather-covered vice grips.

Cam glanced toward Al as she shook the man's

hand. She didn't wince, so she hadn't got the manly test handshake. *Just polite country ways.*

"You told me that those vandals shattered a bat when you put a steel shell around your mailbox," Al said. "That right?"

Haley chuckled, holding a hand up to his face so the chaw filling one cheek wouldn't fall out. "I imagine whoever was swinging that bat is vibrating yet." He laughed again.

"Might even have broken an arm," Al said.

One of Cam's eyebrows rose.

Al's comment struck Haley as funny, and he chuckled some more. When he slowed, Al asked, "You don't have any of what's left of that bat still, do you?"

"Smashed to splinters and toothpicks." Haley laughed. "Might be the butt end left. Out back of that garage over yonder's a big heap of scrap I mean to add to this brush when it's ready to light. I might've throwed it back there. You're welcome to nose around."

"Thanks. We will," Al said.

He and Cam got back into the cruiser. Haley made his slow way back to climb up on his tractor.

Cam didn't speak. She turned into the lane, and they went past the yellow wooden house with a wooden deck that ran all the way around the first floor and hung out over a hill that dropped behind the house. The gravel drive forked, with the left ruts going down the hill and the right sweeping over to a wide shed serving as garage for a truck, with an empty spot where the tractor probably sat, the Bobcat, and a workbench running along one wall with tools and fan belts hanging from the pegboard.

Cam pulled the cruiser up and stopped. They got out and walked around to the back of the building. A chest-high pile of wooden boards, boxes, and pieces of this and that nestled along the back side of the building.

"There it is," Cam said. "Hold on." She went back to the cruiser and returned with a clear plastic evidence bag. She'd slipped on a pair of latex gloves. She reached into the pile and tickled out the broken butt end of a wooden baseball bat. She glanced at it and put it in the bag. "Yep. This one has the *D.V.H.S.*, just like the aluminum bat at the burglary. I wouldn't bet on any prints, though. The old geezer probably carried it and smudged anything we might've gotten."

She put the evidence bag in the trunk, and they both got into the car. Before she started it, she turned to Al. "I thought I told you I was going to solve the burglaries and vandalism case."

"It's yours to solve. Feel free. But did you know about how Toby Buchanan probably got that broken arm?"

"No."

"Then, you're welcome."

She let out a long, slow breath while staring straight ahead. Then she reached forward and turned the key to start the car. "Where to now?"

"I'd like to take a buzz by the Seven Hills Motel. Do you know where it is?"

"I sure do." Her eyes were wide in her quick glance his way. "I thought you didn't think the bone thing was tied to human trafficking?"

"I didn't say anything one way or the other. My mind's still open. I just want to make sure that place isn't still operating."

She frowned, something he was starting to think was her standard look, and drove.

Twenty minutes later, he saw it ahead on the right as they approached the building, same as it'd been the last time he'd seen it: a dilapidated row of rooms with fake stucco, a gutterless ridged tin roof, most doors locked, and windows boarded over. Some windows had been knocked out, and the rooms had been overnight stopping places for the homeless and those looking for someplace dry to smoke crack. What it needed was a wrecking ball swung with repeated vigor.

Cam eased the cruiser over into the gravel parking area.

"I was here when they busted this place." She nodded toward the office at the end. "I can't believe they don't just go around and close everything that looks like this."

"I remember when it was built," Al said. "A young couple, Bob and Peggy, thought it was their dream business, a regular Shangri-La. No one was doing B and Bs then, but they were putting up cheap strip motels. It was far enough from town for the land to be affordable yet close enough to the fishing and boating to be an inexpensive getaway for some."

"Inexpensive?" Cam did that snorting derision thing with her nose that Al thought might well be one of the reasons she was still a single woman.

"Actually, it was quite nice then. Clean. Well painted. Peggy did the landscaping, cleaned the rooms, and Bob did all the maintenance. He told me once that if he hadn't known how to fix air-conditioning units himself, they'd have never made money on the place. They finally sold it and headed back to California, where dreams come with brighter ribbons, I guess."

Cam was still squinting at the place, probably not seeing it in its brighter moments.

"It tried to be a motel for a spell but was hanging on by its teeth. Then we busted a few card games in there, poker, and knew it was turning a better profit, but not legally. Then some call girls worked out of it for a while. Later, it even sunk low enough to be a meth house. That didn't last. It's right out here in the open. Hard for us to miss. Then an Asian woman from Austin bought it, and it seemed to be clean for a while, but a lot of young ladies lived here, and most of the guests were men."

"That was in my era," Cam said. "The Bureau's new human-trafficking team swooped in and busted it open like a bad pumpkin."

"Clayton wasn't too happy about that. We were working it locally, and suddenly there the feds were, clomping about with their hobnail boots."

"I hope that isn't envy. You weren't up to being a Bureau agent, I hear."

"I was sent to Quantico, trained in their work and hand-to-hand. But I never for a moment had a desire to slip on a Hickey Freeman suit and be one of them. I prefer the more cozy county work."

"Speaking of which, this place clearly hasn't stirred in some time. Anyone can see that," she said.

"Where to now, then?"

"You want me to decide?" she asked.

"I'm riding around with you, not vice versa. We could go to the lab and see what Clive has, or we could go to that garage where Toby Buchanan worked and his pal probably still works."

"No." Her face flushed red. The "no" came as close to a shout as he'd heard from her. She caught herself and used her inside-the-car voice.

"What?" He turned toward her.

"I said I wanted to do that one on my own." She was breathing hard but slowed herself. "Okay?"

"Okay, then. Let's go to the lab," he said. "Before we do, let's grab lunch. I know a place. You okay with sushi?"

She nodded, lips pressed tight.

He gave her the address.

She kept her head forward all the way, and he sneaked peeks, like watching a pot boil. He'd studied people all his life, but he'd never run into anyone quite like her, whose waters seemed to run shallow and hard. Something was behind that. He just didn't have a clue about what that might be.

"What's this place?" she asked, pulling the cruiser into the crowded parking lot—a rhetorical question, really, since she could see the large red-and-green neon sign for The Flying Dragon.

He nodded toward the sign.

"A Chinese restaurant? You said we were going to get sushi."

"It's Vietnamese, and we can get sushi. Wait and see."

Al looked around. The parking lot was crowded because a building was going up next door between the Flying Dragon and Dong-Ho Kwon's Korean market, the construction work filling what would have been spillover parking.

He opened the restaurant door for Cam, and she shot inside, where the cool slammed into them after the heat from what was turning out to be the warmest day in some time.

She'd left her white hat in the car but walked tall without it. She held her chin up in a way that reminded Al of a story about Dorothy Parker.

Dorothy had held a door open for Clare Boothe Luce, who instead of going through, waved Dorothy in and said, "Age before beauty."

Dorothy shrugged and went on through. As she passed Clare, she'd said, "Pearls before swine."

Just inside the door, Al and Cam were met by a pretty

young girl in jeans and a white blouse. Al said a couple of quick words to her, and she ushered them to a table beneath a large tank of goldfish.

They sat down.

"Is that what you asked her? To be near the goldfish?" Cam said.

"Yeah."

"I heard a rumor you speak Chinese but don't speak much Spanish. Must be handy, here in the Southwest."

"It's not Chinese. It's Vietnamese. I only speak enough to get me in trouble. A smidgeon. I used up a lot of my stock just saying *goldfish*. What scrap or two I know, I got from my friend Gyp Sing, who owns this place. Here he comes now."

Gyp, a small man with buzzed-short white hair, dressed as usual in a black silk shirt and black pants, carried a tray with a small metal teapot and two cups without handles. He put the tray down on their table and gave Al a nop, which Al stood long enough to return, a slight bow with hands together and thumbs slightly outstretched. He had known Gyp a long time and tried to imagine the first impression Cam was getting. Gyp had dignity in his stride, but when closer, he seemed to be suppressing the grin of someone on the inside of a joke. A dimple showed in one cheek, and his dark eyes twinkled with the merriment of a kid about to get to play bull in a china shop.

"This is Cam." Al waved a hand toward her. He was glad she was wearing a uniform so Al didn't have to listen to the "you a playboy" business from Gyp. Al used to come in with Abbie, and Gyp seemed to think one woman a life was enough.

"Glad you no eat in restaurant Dong-Ho Kwon build."

"It's not done yet. But you'll still get my business, Gyp. It is messing up the parking, though."

"No stray pets now."

"You telling me they'll be the kind of place that'd stir-fry Lassie?"

"Some meat in market now marked. Some not," Gyp said.

"Good thing I lean toward seafood, then."

Gyp said something in Vietnamese, and Al glanced toward Cam before answering. He said just one word in Vietnamese.

"I don't believe you just spoke Vietnamese again, Al," Cam said. She turned to Gyp. "What did he say?"

"He say he not need to buy guns like last time."

Gyp grinned and headed off.

"Was he kidding about that?" Cam said.

"Yeah. Sure he was. You know how the inscrutable mind works."

"Have you ever bought guns from him before?"

"He was just kidding around." Al reached for the pot and poured them each a cup of tea. He looked back up at her. "What?"

"I think your knowing just a tiny dab of Vietnamese is so much bull hooey," she said, reaching for the cup he held out to her. "I begin to think you know more than a few words."

"But still not as much Spanish as I should, as you so kindly pointed out."

Their waitress came out five minutes later and brought them chopsticks, a small squid salad mixed with seaweed for each of them, and a larger plate each of sashimi and pickled ginger, as well as a shrimp and spearmint spring roll—Al's usual.

They ate without speaking. Cam was pretty handy with her chopsticks. Al thought Gyp might have been more circumspect about telling her what he had asked. Cam couldn't otherwise have figured it out on her own.

Gyp waited until they were done before he came back to their table. He must have been watching them through the peephole in the kitchen door, because as soon as they put down their chopsticks and while Cam was still dabbing at her mouth with her napkin, he came striding across the room toward them.

He pulled out a chair and sat down across from Al and said something.

"Better keep it in English." Al nodded toward Cam.

Gyp nodded and gave her a nop from where he sat. She didn't seem to know quite what to do, so she nodded back.

He turned back to Al and waited.

"We went by the Seven Hills Motel today. It's as closed up as a ghost town. Hasn't reopened," Al said.

"And?" Gyp's eyes flicked to Cam then back to Al.

"They arrested Hin Lee Yang. Has anyone replaced her in that sort of business?"

"What happen to tall red-hair lady you with last time?"

"Fergie? She's fine. Back at the house. It's not about that. I'm not looking for myself. I just want to know where the action went."

"Action not good for you."

"I know. Again, it's not for me. Hin Lee Yang was working out of an apartment complex for a while until there were complaints about too much coming and going."

"Inning and outing if you ask me," Gyp said.

"By men," Al continued. Having a conversation with Gyp was sometimes elusive. He was fond of playing cat and mouse with the subject. Al usually let him, which was why they got along.

"You know what I mean. When she got run out of the apartment complex, she bought the motel. Then the cops raided and took that down. You know anyone running a similar setup, where the girls come in, stay all the time, don't have papers?"

"White slaves?" Gyp said. "Only this time, not round eye?"

Al thought he caught Gyp barely suppressing a grin. He was showing off or acting silly, maybe because a lady was present.

"Yeah," Al said.

"You might try Red Barn."

"That the place off Dessau Road?"

Gyp nodded. He stood, waved to the waitress on the far side of the restaurant, turned to trade nops with Al, then went off at a brisk walk across the room, apparently done speaking.

"You have an unorthodox way of detecting," Cam said.

"And yet I get results."

"I checked," she said begrudgingly. "Best record in the department."

He stood up and gestured toward the Restrooms sign. "Don't forget. I'm not in the department anymore, and records are made to be broken. I'll be right back." He took off at a brisk walk.

When he came out of the short restroom corridor that also led to the kitchen, he paused for a moment, able to see Cam still sitting at their table. She put away a cell phone.

The kitchen door to his left swung open a foot, and Gyp let just his face show. "She okay, Al?" he asked.

"I don't know yet. We'll see."

———◇———

When Al and Cam came into the lab, Al saw Clive bent over a table washed with light at the center of the room. He'd arranged the bones the way he wanted them. Teddy stood across the table, occasionally reaching out to move one of the bone bits back into a line the way she wanted, and he'd have to return it to the way he wanted. She giggled.

When they came into the room, Teddy looked up, starting to smile, but saw Cam and lowered her head. The giggling stopped.

"What do you make of it?" Al asked. He stopped beside Clive and looked down at the separate collections of bone.

"Just got them back," he said. "I'm having another look at them myself."

"Back from where?" Cam asked.

Clive ignored her.

"These are all separate victims?" Al counted seven groups of bones.

"Yep."

"All Asian?"

"Nope. I thought that might be the case after the skull was ID'd. But we've got a mix here."

"Of what?" Al asked.

"Who looked at the bones?" Cam asked.

Clive looked at Al. "Asian. Hispanic. And, dammit, Russian."

"Russian?"

"Ukrainian, I'm told."

"Did the FBI look at these?" Cam asked. "If so, you wouldn't have them back." She realized she'd answered her own question.

Both Al and Clive looked at her.

"We're trying to see what we have before we make a big ado," Al said.

"Is that the procedure?"

"It is for now until we know what we've stepped into," Al said.

"How's Clayton feel about that?" Cam stared down at the bones.

"He's okay with it for now." The deep voice boomed over the sound of the door closing. Clayton stood just inside the door. He wore a blue suit and a red tie and carried his white hat in one hand at his side. "How big a bomb is this, Clive?"

"It's ticking. That's for sure."

"Any thoughts, Al?"

"Oh, I have thoughts. None that lead anywhere for sure yet."

"I have an idea," Cam said. "Isn't there a task force on human trafficking?"

"Do you absolutely know for sure that's what you have here?" Clayton asked. He walked across the room and looked down at the bones. "Howdy, Teddy."

She looked up, shared a quick half grin, glanced toward Cam, and lowered her head again.

Al was watching Cam. At least she didn't get all soft and sycophantic in the presence of her boss. Clayton didn't get hands-on with all the staff. He had majors and captains for that. But he did like to mingle with the few detectives and thus "keep a feel for the pulse of the county's underbelly." *His words.*

"We don't know anything for sure," Al said, "yet."

Clayton towered over Cam. She looked up at him without a flinch.

"I know what the task force is working on," Clayton said. "I'd like you two to follow your own noses for the moment. If your paths cross, then I'll deal with that then. I'd like to have a couple of separate brains and eyes working this for now."

"Kind of unusual for you to leave your office and come

out to look into a case. Is there anything we should know about?" Cam asked.

Clive's eyes widened, and Al knew his own eyebrows probably rose a bit, giving him away. He couldn't fault Cam for a lack of audacity. No wonder she wanted to hop right to the top spot. Going up the ladder might prove to be a chore for her.

The corner of Clayton's mouth twitched into a momentary grin. "You're a detective. Detect." He spun and headed for the door. Just before he opened it, he turned back and asked Cam, "How are you coming along with those burglaries?"

"Making progress," she said.

He nodded and went out the door.

As soon as the door closed behind him, Cam said, "He just has us wear white hats because he thinks it makes us look like Texas Rangers."

Before Al could comment, his cell phone rang. He held up a finger and stepped away until he was on the other side of the table. He recognized the number.

"What is it, Gyp?" Al spoke low.

"Van parked down the street. Watch restaurant."

"Who is it, do you think?"

"I don't know. Agents. Look like ATF to me."

"Oh. Really?"

"Don't come back," Gyp said.

"We'll talk."

"No. No talk. I mean it. Don't come back." Gyp hung up, leaving Al with a dial tone buzzing in his ear while he stared across the table of bones at his partner.

CHAPTER EIGHT

"**W**HAT'S THE MATTER WITH YOU? You look like someone who just lost a friend."

Al heard the glass door slide shut behind Fergie as she came out onto the back porch that extended from the second floor. She came over to stand beside him, where he leaned forward in the dark, forearms on the railing. He heard a low whine and glanced back inside to see Bonnie tugging Tanner away from the door by the collar. Bonnie led the dog past the brightly lit dining area, but he did not seem to want to go gently into that good night. To the left, in the kitchen, Maury was getting a long-necked bottle of Dos Equis amber out of the refrigerator.

"I may well have," Al said.

"Who?"

"Gyp Sing."

"You've known him for years and years. What happened?"

Thunder rumbled. He knew it to be the night when in early May the biggest full moon of the year coincided with the moon's perigee, its closest approach to Earth. Its annual visit usually played hob with the tides as well as the level of criminal and just plain antic behavior. Domestic quarrels and bar fights went off the charts, and squad cars were kept busy buzzing here and there. So far, the evening had been too cloudy for Al to see the moon, though he could make out the ripple and chop of waves from wind gusting across the lake that spread out behind the house. The thunder had been rolling nearer, and the damp felt closer. Flashes of yellow-white lightning burst and spread out close to the clouds. *All that sound and flashing, and still no rain.*

Tanner whined again inside—whether from wanting to be outside with Al or in fear of the thunder, Al couldn't say. Bonnie and Maury were talking to the dog the way people do who don't know exactly what they should be saying.

"Do you recall that time you and I went to Gyp's restaurant and picked up a couple of guns?"

"I haven't forgotten a single detail of that whole episode of our lives."

"Well, Cam and I went there so I could see if he had any leads now that Hin Lee Yang and the Seven Hills Motel are closed down."

"A very nice thing, that place closing," Fergie said. "I hope they never let her back out. A very evil little woman."

"The point is, in the conversation, Gyp asks if I want to buy any more guns, this right in front of Cam. Next thing I know, I'm getting an infuriated call from Gyp not to ever darken his door again since he thinks ATF agents are staking out his place now."

"Not a coincidence?"

"Sure doesn't look like one. Nothing I can prove, though."

"You think Cam made the call?"

"I'm not sure what to think. All I know is that Gyp is genuinely pissed."

"He's been a good friend of yours. He'll forgive you... in time."

"Maybe. Be that as it may, Cam's the potential loose cannon who worries me."

"You think Clayton had you two joined at the hip for some insightful reason, you being the resident loose cannon of the department in the past?"

"I don't know what Clayton's up to, and I don't know what Cam's up to. But some stale Limburger from Denmark springs to mind."

"But you're making progress on your case?"

"Still looking for a place to put in one end of the crowbar, but I am starting to think such a place may exist."

Tanner gave a short, quick bark inside. He rarely ever barked. Al recognized it as his *"hey, pay attention"* bark. Bonnie was inside with a chew toy, trying to lure Tanner away from the sliding glass door to play games.

"She's giving us time to chat." Fergie leaned forward to press against the rail beside Al. "Seems none of us get time to really talk to each other."

"Well, there are always those snuggle moments when you two make it past my watchdog. What's up with that? I'm sure you two have discussed that, almost certainly at greater length than I care to know."

"Aw, that's just harmless fun, Al. We neither one want much, and certainly not a man full-time. We just like the feel of being pressed up to a naked human. The sense of connection."

"You've got each other."

"But, alas, we neither bat left-handed. We don't want more than the manly holding and pressing. Well, maybe Bonnie might go farther if encouraged."

"And I haven't encouraged."

"So I hear. What else is worrying you?"

Al sighed, but it was lost in the loudest clap of thunder yet. He mentally counted *Mississippi*s before he saw the flash from the lightning—three miles away and coming his way at a fast pace.

"Well, I look out at the lake and wonder how long we're going to have fresh drinking water that's worth a damn," he said. "I've heard that if we don't stop harvesting the sea at the current pace, we'll have completely depleted the ocean's fisheries by 2050. I worry the pundits are right about that. I worry the gasoline companies are bleeding us dry and there's nothing we can do about it. And I worry about politicians who say they want to 'grow' the economy, only their way of doing that is by pouring on more of their kind of manure. The bulk of the growing that interests them seems to happen in their own pockets."

"Ah, and here I thought you weren't paying too much attention to the world," she said.

"How did your first day on the job go with Doug Chandle? Do you have a pretty lively case?"

"I don't know about that. I'm not absolutely sure we have a case at all."

"How so?" he asked.

"The client's a hospital, but we have to meet the administrator off site. Real hush-hush."

"What's the beef? Someone helping himself or herself to the medicinal supplies?"

"I wish."

Al waited, knowing she'd get to it when ready.

"The thing is," she said, "it doesn't even make sense on the surface of it. The administrator, at the number-two position in the hospital, has us checking out a doctor."

"Crooked as a bent corkscrew?"

"Not at all. Everything Doug was able to gather has the man coming out a saint. That's why he brought me in. Thought a woman's touch would help."

"Will it?"

"I doubt it."

The rain clouds suddenly burst like someone twisting

94

on the shower knob. Since the breeze had been in their faces, they both spun to race inside. Tanner shot across the room to leap at Al, giving him the old pawing and licking, as if to say, *"Thought you were never going to return. Ever. Ever."*

———◆———

Al looked over the neighborhood as Cam pulled the cruiser up in front of a house that sat so close to the extreme edge of the Del Valle school district that the principal some years back had pondered whether Donnie Farris should go there. Al got the impression, in digging up that tidbit, that the principal wished Donnie had gone almost any other direction.

Al glanced toward Cam as she got out of the cruiser, uniform as stiff and starchy as ever. She put on her hat. He hadn't gotten a single word from her yet that day, so he didn't get the opportunity to ask if she had sicced the ATF on Gyp Sing. She sure wasn't acting any different from usual, but that didn't mean much. She wasn't much of a sharer and liked to play her cards close.

The house had been painted a dark brown, covering some sort of horizontal wood-simulating siding, asbestos for all Al could tell. The roof was tin, and the chimney was missing a couple bricks. A two-vehicle carport was crowded with one old red van with four flat tires, a washer and dryer, and two clotheslines filled with work clothes. The front yard looked to be mostly dirt with a few tufts of fescue grass fighting a losing battle with foot traffic amid the tire prints of a vehicle that apparently parked in the front yard when it was there. Someone had shoved a row of yellow plastic flowers into the ground along the front. Their petals were covered in a light dusting of dirt, and they did little to cheer up the place.

The door was open a foot, and a small pug came to stand in the gap at the bottom and growl in a low and earnest way.

Cam rapped on the sill of the door. "Sheriff's department. Are you here, Mrs. Farris?"

"Sampson. You get back of there. Hear?" The woman's shout sounded as if she'd just swallowed gravel.

The loop end of a leash slashed through the air and slapped the bottom doorsill with a crack. The pug spun and darted back inside.

"Okay. It's safe to come in now."

Cam looked at Al, shrugged, and pushed the door open. The woman, Mrs. Farris, sat in a brown cloth recliner across from an old-fashioned television with a deep back and a small digital converter box sitting on top. The sound was off, though a soap opera flickered on the imperfect screen. The dog's leash had been tied to the metal leg of a small dining table behind her chair. She wore a housedress, loose and falling around her like a brown waterfall. She was skinny, her flesh a deathly pale-bluish hue. Al recognized the smell in the room at once. Past the traces of stale sweat and dust, he got the cloud of years of unfiltered Camels being smoked. He'd once had a partner who smoked them in the car. It was a smell he didn't mind all that much, and it was probably far better than what it was masking. Beside Mrs. Farris's chair sat an ashtray on a side table, piled high with squashed butts.

"What do you people want?" she rasped. She pulled a fresh pack out of a carton next to the ashtray and tamped one end of the pack against the chair's arm.

Cam stepped closer and handed her a warrant. She'd had to make a pretty strong case with Judge Wilkinson to get it, but Cam looked neither proud nor happy as she handed it over. Al wondered for the flash of a second if anything ever made the woman happy.

"We need to look around," Cam said.

Mrs. Farris barely opened the document. She glanced at it, folded it back the way it'd been, and crumpled it in the middle as she held it in a right fist she waved up at Cam. "Why can't you people just leave him the hell alone? He's a good enough boy, maybe a wee bit ornery but as good a son as I could want or deserve. His father was nothing to shake a stick at, but the boy's okay. Can't you leave him be?"

"Do you think he might have gotten mixed up with a bad crowd?" Cam asked.

"I know, you're picking on Toby, too. Another fine boy. He'd live with his mother too, like Donnie, except the good Lord took her young. His daddy died from drink, but the boy's okay. Left the kid a place to stay, anyways. Why can't you leave him be?"

Cam looked at Al and shrugged. She started toward an open bedroom door. "That's my bedroom," the woman shouted, her raspy voice up an octave. Her Zippo clicked shut, and the evidence of a new burning coffin nail floated through the air.

Cam went past a bathroom Al didn't even want to enter and opened the other door that was closed. She turned to Al. "I can do this. Don't expect to find much. Though it'd be great if he hasn't sold any of the stuff from the burglaries. Why don't you wait outside and make sure he doesn't come home and surprise me digging through his junk?"

Al looked inside the door she'd just opened, seeing an untidy mess and catching the odor of someone not overly keen about personal hygiene or changing sheets. He spun on a heel and headed for the front door.

"Lousy coppers," the lady muttered as he passed by, making her sound like an extra from a 1930s movie. Maybe she *was* that old. She looked it, but that could have been the smoke that had wrinkled and aged her like a pile of parchment leather.

When he glanced back at her, before he went out through the front door, her mouth pressed tight, and two angry spears of white smoke shot out of her nostrils at different angles, yet her eyes flinched the way you'd see in a puppy that had been abused when young. Anything like anger he felt sifted out of him like sand pouring from his ankles.

Outside, he took a deep breath. *My God, the air smells good outside after that. Cam can have the inside digging.*

She wasn't much of a team player. He could see that. Years back, when his colleagues were kidding around, they'd bought him a Warner Brothers coffee mug with the image of the Tasmanian devil and the message "Doesn't play well with others." He thought about digging through his junk to see if he could find that mug and pass it on to Cam, though she didn't seem to have much of a sense of humor either. He guessed he couldn't kick when he reminded himself why he'd been given the mug.

When his partner Barrett's brains had gotten sprayed up the side of Skid Stoker's house that time, Al worked alone for a while and rather enjoyed it. Maybe he was alone because of what he did to Skid once he wrenched a shotgun away from him—hadn't been pretty. Maybe Fergie was right. He'd been something of a loose cannon for Clayton in his own day.

He was deciding whether to stay where he was or go sit in the car when an aged blue Ford Ranger with a red driver's-side door pulled up across the street from the Farris house. He expected Donnie to come leaping out and rush toward the house. When the driver sat there, staring through the open window toward him, he walked out to the truck and leaned an arm on its top to look in at the driver.

"Well, Toby Buchanan, what brings you this way?"

Toby looked up at Al and smiled. *Big mistake.* Al was immediately hypnotized by looking at those teeth. Mouth aside, Toby was a lanky post–high school bit of driftwood with three days of black stubble on his lanky chin and cheeks. His eyes were a little close together, his hair tousled and black, and he had the yellowish pallor of someone who usually stayed indoors, smoking, or who only prowled around at night, up to antics not quite as attractive as those of a vampire bat. But his teeth had the ability to transfix Al's stare even though Al was saying over and over in his own mind, *"Don't stare at the teeth. Don't stare at the teeth."*

The teeth were narrow and green in color, with plenty of space between them, and each tooth had a waist, narrower in the middle. They were like baby teeth that had stayed around for a hardscrabble life in a mouth that was a stranger to brushing, flossing, and mouthwash. Al was grateful for the breeze whipping past the truck's open window. He stared at the teeth.

Toby's right arm was in a cast. It was one of the newer kind, made of synthetic materials, none of the white plaster of Al's youth. The cast was already as dirty as the arm that rested on the driver's windowsill.

"You think it's easy driving a stick with only one good arm?" Toby asked.

"Into each life some rain must fall," Al said. "How'd you break it?"

"Fell."

"Hmm."

"Why're you messing with Donnie's place?"

Al had reverted to staring at Toby's teeth. *Good gad.* He'd also been wondering about Donnie's place when Cam got the warrant. If he'd been a criminal the age of those boys, he'd have a shack or hideout or, as was common, a rental storage unit where he could keep anything incriminating. He thought they should check the ones closest to their homes, maybe check a few pawnshops that had been caught fencing. When he'd started to suggest that approach, Cam had cut him off, insisting again that this case was hers alone. *Fine with me.* He cared a lot more about the bones in the dog shelters. She could thrash around a bit with that burglary and vandalism mess.

"I see your point, Toby—two fine young upstanding lads like yourselves."

"Ha," Toby said, in spite of himself.

Al was thinking through Freudian slips he should avoid, like "the tooth of it."

"How're you getting by without a job and... medical plan?" Al asked. *Damn.* He'd nearly said *dental plan.* "Still living in your late dad's double-wide?"

Toby's grin turned surly, like a dog that'd been kicked.

"Hey," Cam yelled. She came out the front door of the Farris place.

Al turned to look that way when he heard the truck shift into gear. He spun back in time to see Toby's left arm return from the gearshift to the steering wheel. Toby grinned at Al with his mouthful of evil teeth. Al stepped back as the truck pulled away from the curb. Toby was careful not to chirp the tires, though he probably would have really enjoyed peeling out with a squeal and the smell of burning black rubber.

"Who was that?" Cam asked as Al climbed into the cruiser.

"Just an interested citizen making sure we weren't harassing the villagers."

"Get out of here. That was Toby Buchanan."

"If you knew," Al asked, "then why'd you ask?"

CHAPTER NINE

"DO YOU THINK CLAYTON IS going a bit crazy? I'm not sure this woman should be a cop, and I know I should be out to pasture, retired." Al ducked beneath a mountain cedar limb that hung low over the path. He pulled the limb out of the way for Fergie, who followed.

Fergie held the end of Tanner's leash, but the little fellow liked to walk close to Al, which led to him wrapping the leash around Al's legs every few steps.

Al bent to untangle himself and got licked on both hands by Tanner, who a second later took off to tug Fergie toward some interesting aroma along the deer path that led from Al's yard through the empty lot next to his place. He'd bought the lot a while back when he was on salary so no one could build near him.

"I believe your little one may have attention disorder issues," Fergie said.

"No. Dogs are like that. These walks are his chance to read the area newspaper with his nose. He just saw a bold headline on page two." Al glanced up. "It's going to be dark soon."

"Mmm."

"You getting anywhere on your case?" he asked.

She gave the leash a tug when Tanner wanted to roll in something that probably smelled bad. "The doctor transplanted a liver today and saved a young man's life.

Now, if that doesn't make him out to be an arch villain, I don't know what does."

Al glanced her way. "Bonnie's the one who suggested you and I take a walk. Is she giving up, trying to foist me your way?"

"You'd better not start thinking like that, or she's apt to leap out of nowhere, hogtie you, and have her way with you."

"And I used to live in such a quiet house."

"Alone."

"Your point?"

"Oh, come on. Your life is fuller now, more complex. Admit it." Fergie barely suppressed an outright grin.

"Oh, it's more complex. What if I don't want complex?"

"After all your years in the department, you'd go bonkers if you were forced to do nothing but fish and loaf."

"I might like a chance to try that. Yet here I am working again, and with a woman I'm not sure about."

"You didn't have to say yes when Clayton asked you to mentor a detective. But I know you. You'd always do a favor for Clayton. It's the woman that rubs your rhubarb the wrong way. What would you change about her?"

"Well, her procedure's a little shaky."

"I'll bet your approach seems equally odd to her. You always seem to know someone who you can go to as the back door to information. She hasn't been around as long as you, enough to seem to know half the county. Plus, you're a wealth of useless tidbits of information that only occasionally help with a case."

"You mean like the can opener was invented forty-eight years after cans first came into use. I wake up wondering where I heard about the Wapishana tribe, did they ever find Prester John, and whatever became of the Colossus of Rhodes. Then I remember. It's not necessarily a good thing."

"You're singing to the choir, Al. And that's just the kind of esoteric info that might lead someone to kosh you upside the head with a brick. Let's stick with her procedural skills."

"She seems to stab instead of being thorough, methodical."

"Like you?"

"Like me. Like Clayton. Like every other detective in the department."

"It rubs you more that she might have called in an outside agency, doesn't it?"

"Yeah. We pride ourselves in not having to call the Texas Rangers or the FBI every time we get a case where the waters are deep. I understand why small counties lean that way, but we don't need or want outside help."

"Those sound like Clayton's words and only yours as his favorite son. Look, I was in the city PD for years, and we called out for an assist often. Sometimes, that's the proper and effective way to go."

"Well, in the county, we don't like to do that."

"Good thing this isn't about ego," Fergie muttered.

———◆———

"What the hell're you eating?" Cam's brow tightened into two deep furrows.

"This? Beef jerky. My dog loves the stuff, but I'm not sure it's good for him." Al took another bite.

"Do you know what chemicals are used to process it?"

"I have a pretty fair idea."

"And yet you munch on."

"I'm going to miss out on Bonnie's comfort-food cooking night, and we have a long stretch ahead of us."

Cam let out a puff of air and turned to look out the closed window of the 1997 Olds Cutlass, her get-around car when not on duty. Clayton had offered them one of the department's unmarked cars, but Cam had told him they get too readily known by the wrong element. That had raised one of Clayton's eyebrows toward Al.

Al had picked up a tall cup of coffee and the beef jerky when she'd stopped for gas. He favored junk food when on a stakeout. She'd curled a lip and gotten nothing. The coffee might've been a bad choice, come later, when an inevitable bathroom break would roll around. Because of that need to open a door later, he'd gotten her to turn off the dome light. He realized he'd never been on a stakeout with a female partner before. They didn't beat up the air with any excessive chatter about football, fishing, or anything interesting to a female, either. They'd had some pretty longish blocks of silence.

"Why did they name it Red Barn? It doesn't look like a barn." She was staring across at their target, a low wooden building with an arching center foyer.

It had been painted red, but since the light had faded some time before, they could no longer make that out.

She turned to him, making eye contact, then as quickly turned inward. He hadn't figured out if he scared her or disgusted her or if she just liked the inside of her own head better. She lifted her binoculars and looked out toward the parking lot. A pickup was pulling in.

"It started out life as a dance hall, a two-stepping honky-tonk kicker bar with a big dusted hardwood-floor dance area," he said. "Thing is, way out here, it was too far to go for anyone but the locals, and the demographic was all wrong for this place ever making it as that. You get a bunch of liquored-up cowhand types out here, and the owner's big cost turned out to be security. Plenty of fights in the parking lot, and one woman got raped in her parked car. Place closed down for a while and opened back up as a flea market on Saturdays. Couldn't generate enough revenue for that in the long haul. So now, who do you think drives all the way out here to this place?"

She didn't need to answer. Out of every car or truck arriving in the parking lot, a man got out—sometimes two—and one time, six men climbed out of what looked like a Town Car on what was possibly a road-trip bachelor party or just some group idea of a good time.

Cam didn't grind her teeth, but her silence grew profound for stretches.

Al found himself watching the former honky-tonk and not focusing on the men coming in and out. He was picturing the way the building had been. Seemed to him that every little part of the county had started with good intentions but often took a wrong turn at the light. The Seven Hill Motel had started with that dream of Bob and Peggy to run a cozy motel that offered a service, a fishing-camp hangout near the lake. It had ended the way of this place, a dance hall where once-happy couples two-stepped to the country swing of Bob Wills, Ray Benson, or any number of other performers. The people had been happy, most of them, but the only thing going on in there currently was probably a whole lot of happy endings.

"How did this place slip under the department's radar?" Cam asked after a long quiet spell.

"Well, it didn't entirely. These places pop up and then disappear. But they don't get visible on their own until there are a few calls, disturbances, and this place has had none. That hints at a very good security team."

"Hmm." The ominous sound suggested that she thought some deputies somewhere were slacking or maybe even taking payoffs.

Heaven help the department if she ever got the whip in her hand.

"How are you coming with those burglaries?" he asked.

"We know those pinheads Toby and Donnie have graduated from vandalism to larceny. At least, I do. I don't think they can climb any higher on the food chain than that. But I'd like to be able to lock them both away just the same. Clayton says I need more than I've got."

"You searched their houses. Got nothing. If I was you, I'd get a recent picture of each from their school yearbook and go around to the storage-facility units nearest to their homes, then work outward."

"Well, I'm not you, and I don't need your help on the merest routine detail." Her mouth clamped tight, but she was clearly digesting and planning.

He suspected she might just try what he'd suggested on her own in the morning.

"You think I'm dense or something, don't you?" she asked. "Or at least bull-headed stubborn."

"I don't think that at all," he lied. He suspected she was smart enough, but she must've been a pill in school when anyone tried to teach her anything.

A long stretch of quiet settled in the car, with him wondering how soon was too soon to go for his bathroom break.

She spoke next. "Why do men even come to places like this?"

"You know. A married man told me it was to get the kinds of things he couldn't get at home."

"Hmpf." When he said nothing, she finally said, "I suppose you have that all taken care of at your place. Don't you have two women living there with you? At least that's the scuttlebutt in the department."

"It's not like you'd think. Did the scuttlebutt mention my brother's living there, too?"

"I'm surprised you don't have something hot going on—someone who looks the way you do, even at your advanced age."

"Gee, thanks. I think. You aren't making a pass at me, are you, Cam?"

"Heaven forbid. I mean you're not a gargoyle, so I just figured there must be some lonely old broads out there to whom you might seem like arm candy. Women start heating up at that age."

His head snapped toward her then panned back to the Red Barn. The car grew quiet again, a deep, heavy quiet he didn't care to break.

Al turned off the porch light, and the minute the glass door outside turned into a mirror, Tanner saw his reflection and barked. He rushed toward it. Al slid the door open, and Tanner raced out onto the porch. *Nothing.* Al could see it baffled the little fellow. *"Where did that other dog go?"* So Al went out and leaned on the railing to look across the light-speckling waves on the lake while Tanner sniffed in every corner as he made a circuit of the porch. *"That dog has to be somewhere out here."*

The door slid open, and Maury came outside.

"Well?"

"Well what?"

"Bonnie or Fergie?"

"You know I haven't picked and don't intend to, at least as far as I know."

"Are you afraid you'll anger one if you pick the other?"

"Hell, Maury. You think I'm playing chess when I'm playing backgammon."

"I don't understand."

"I'm not trying to swoop in on either one of them."

"I still don't understand."

"That's what makes me interesting to them and you... well, not."

"You think it's because you're playing hard to get?"

"Like I said. I'm not playing hard to get. I *am* hard to get."

"Ah, saving yourself for that new partner. Is that it?"

"Touching on that, Maury, we're looking at some sort of house of ill repute. We might need someone to go inside and look around."

"I'll throw myself on that hand grenade."

"I haven't even told you what I want you to do."

"I heard 'house of ill repute.' I'm in. One question. Expense account?"

"I was thinking we might use someone else."

"I said I'd do it. Don't take this away from me, Al."

"I don't want to put you at risk."

"I don't mind."

"All I really need is for someone to go inside, get a good look around, and then come right back out. No purchases, no activity."

"We'll see about that."

Before Al could respond, Fergie slid the glass door open a foot. Tanner shot inside. *"Maybe that other dog is in there."*

The dark outside and light inside gave him a show. Fergie wore a diaphanous red nightgown Al could see right through. He heard Maury swallow next to him.

"Are you coming to bed, Al?" she said.

"What?"

"It's my night. Bonnie and I have come to an agreement."

"An agreement about what?"

"Oh, come on. I'll explain."

Al pushed away from the railing, headed for the sliding glass door.

"What about me?" Maury said.

"Don't go down there," Fergie said. "She's liable to tear your head off."

"Well, then, Al. Don't forget about using me to scout."

"We'll see."

"Oh, Al. Don't toy with me!"

"What's that about?" Fergie said.

"Aw, he was just wanting to know more about what it is I do."

CHAPTER TEN

A L EASED HIS BASS BOAT up to the dock, tied its front tender, and fastened a stern line to cleats on the dock before lifting Tanner up. Tanner moved across the dock's surface from corner to corner, sniffing around, casing the area while Al got his catch of crappies out of the live well into a fish basket. He'd stopped catching when he had eight nice black crappies that would make a good lunch. *Man, it was nice to have the morning off to himself since he'd be back on stakeout tonight.*

Midmorning, while fishing for bass, he'd caught one nice crappie and decided to go after a mess. His grandfather had insisted that a good fisherman could smell a school of crappies. Al had caught that particular oily fish smell in the breeze, enough to encourage him to switch to a small yellow jig. Lifting and bobbing the lure in the unseen deep took him back to being a boy again. *Innocence? Hah!* Crappies tended to school near structures, underwater trees or changes in the rocky sides or bottom of a lake. He'd stayed right in that one spot until he'd caught enough for lunch, then he'd stopped.

When he fished for bass, he always turned them loose because they were overfished enough, and he hoped to keep their population steady. Then he went to the store and bought cod or haddock or sockeye salmon and wondered about any irony in turning fish loose and then spending money on fish. Plus, he knew the fisheries of the oceans were getting hit hard. But crappie and bluegill had sustainable populations that needed to be fished, so he didn't mind bring a mess of either of those panfish home. In fact, he looked forward to the sound of the sizzling skillet.

Being out on the lake alone—except for Tanner, who was as content to stare out at the lake as Al—gave him time to think, getting everything into context and perspective. Maybe he was winding up about Cam over nothing or very little. The ATF sniffing around Gyp could have been a coincidence. He decided to maintain an open mind.

While Tanner stayed on the dock, keeping an eye on the fish basket, Al moved the bass boat over to the electric lift and hoisted it up under its protective roof. Then he got out his cleaning board and fish knife. He filleted out his catch, putting the fillets into a pan of saltwater from the kitchen. Tanner crowded close, curious and sniffing, but he didn't interfere, just watching with the fascination to detail only canine eyes can show.

Inside, Bonnie had already prepared what she needed and rinsed off each fillet, dipped it into an egg wash, rolled it in a mix of flour, cornmeal, and spices, then dropped it into Al's biggest iron skillet, where it popped and spattered. He was pretty sure she favored using bacon fat or lard for the process, which he hated to admit was only going to make lunch taste better. She was wearing her apron over jeans and one of her nursing-scrubs tops.

Fergie had a salad ready and was putting together a classic vinaigrette dressing, complete with a dollop of Dijon mustard. She wore tighter jeans and a white peasant blouse that took the emphasis off how slender she looked when standing by Bonnie.

"How come you're not out detecting with Doug Chandle

today?" Al paused in pouring himself a cup of coffee to ask her.

"I'm not sure there's even anything going on there. The guy just put new kidneys in a woman who was right up to the finish line of when it was going to be too late. Doug flew off to do a background check where the doctor worked before."

"Can't you just do that on the Internet these days?"

"Not and get anything gritty, the way colleagues and others felt, what the man was like to work around. The guy is squeaky clean so far. Makes me wonder why the hospital is wasting its money."

"What *is* that smell?" Maury came out of Al's room in a robe, rubbing his hair with a towel. "It's wonderful."

He might have been sleeping on the couch, but he still liked to use Al's shower. It had large brown tiles on the floor, walls, and ceiling, and it even had a bench for sitting. With its glass door, it was what Kinky Friedman called a "rain room."

"You boys are going to need a hearty meal if you're going to be out playing late," Bonnie said. "I only wish I could go along. But someone's gonna have to hold down the fort. Maybe when Al comes in, I'll be the one gets to rattle his bones like maracas."

Al glanced toward Fergie. She might have seen apprehension on his face, for she winked.

"Are you sure you're up for this?" Fergie asked Maury.

Maury moved closer to watch Bonnie make a few hush puppies by dropping them to deep-fry in the sizzling lard. He nodded.

Al said, "I believe it was Hemingway who said, 'The world breaks everyone, and afterward, some are strong at the broken places.' I think Maury is up to an active role of at least nosing around. Just so long as he doesn't decide to plunk down the butter-and-egg money for the favors available in there."

"Maybe that wouldn't be a risk," Maury said, "if I was the one getting any attention at home."

Bonnie turned from her spattering skillet and patted Maury's wet head. "You just wait, honey. Your turn will come."

Al lowered his binoculars and took a sip of coffee. *No beef jerky tonight.* He hadn't decided whether getting some would just irritate Cam or not, and he had deferred on the side of trying to get along better. He wondered whether the problem was with him.

"Look at all these guys pouring into this place. What do you bet more than half of them are married?" she asked. "Hell, most of them." The hour was early enough in the afternoon to still be light, dusk. The dark of evening was an hour or two away, yet business was picking up at the Red Barn.

Al's thoughts were elsewhere. He sometimes wondered what Davy Crockett, Colonel Travis, Jim Bowie, and the others who'd fought in the Alamo would think if they could see modern-day Texas. Maybe a good old-fashioned bawdy house would seem attractive to some of the men, especially Bowie—not Travis and Crockett, not the way he pictured them.

"Were you ever married?" Cam said.

"Once. A long time ago."

"What happened?"

"I don't want to talk about it." He knew it to be a long and not uninteresting story, but it involved Maury, and not all of the sting had dissipated. He didn't want to tell her he hadn't talked to Maury for twenty years over it.

"Well, I can tell you I caught my husband cheating. Only once. It's all it took. He cried and wanted to make it right, to work on it, even to go to marriage counseling. I told him, 'Pack up your things, or as God is my witness, I'll rent a wood chipper and put everything of yours through it, including you.'"

"Did you love him when you married him?"

"That's a stupid question. Of course I did... or had at least deluded myself I had."

"Could you ever love again?"

"I sure hope you're not asking on behalf of yourself."

He paused to sort through a handful of responses, ranging from "Are you kidding?" to "I can't even conceive of an instance where that could be possible."

He settled for and said out loud, "No. I'm sure you have plenty of young men your own age interested."

"As if I would give any of those dim bulbs a chance. I think I'm done with that sort of thing unless I come across some guy who's deaf, dumb, and financially and physically well endowed. Then I might think about it."

He came up with a half dozen responses to that and shared none of them. They sat in quiet for a while.

Al finally asked, "Are you doing any good with your burglary investigation?"

"You mean other than knowing who's behind a number of the burglaries but not being able to prove a damn thing?" She let out a harsh puff of air. "Took a school yearbook around to four storage facilities near Toby's house. Got a pop on the fourth. Manager recognized Toby, commented on the teeth even though Toby's mouth is closed in the school picture. It was enough, along with what we already had, for a warrant."

"And?"

"Do you remember that time Geraldo Rivera took a film

crew down into Al Capone's basement, expecting to find treasures?"

"They found nothing. It turned into a major media embarrassment and a scathing indictment against live reality television."

"It was like that. Popped the lock with bolt cutters, swung the door open, and not a thing."

"Hmm." Al wasn't surprised. Toby and Donnie might have been somewhat dense petty criminals, but they weren't idiots. Searching their cribs had alerted them.

"Now, I'm back to square one, and Clayton doesn't seem happy about it. He asked what you thought, and I told him I'd given you the morning off so you'd be fresh for tonight."

"It's true I'm not as young as I once was."

They went back to silent mode for a while. Al sat up straighter when he saw his own truck pull into the parking lot.

"Hey, for the first time," Cam said. "A woman in the truck. She's driving, but the guy's getting out. What the hell? You think it might be a wife buying her husband a birthday gift? I can't imagine."

Al hoped she wouldn't run the plate. Maury walked across to the front door with far more eagerness than Al cared to see.

Cam kept her glasses on Maury all the way to the front door. Only when he'd entered and the door had swung shut behind him did she lower the binoculars. "If I found out my husband had even gone to a place like this, that would have been it. But for a wife to take her husband here? Incredible!"

Al could have touched on some assumptions she was making or could have let her spin. But once he thought about it, he decided he'd better clue her in.

"That's my guy," he said. "I sent him in to see what he could find out. I might be recognized going in there, but he won't. I hope."

She spun and shouted at a volume enhanced by being in the small space of her car. "You arranged to have someone go in there without telling me!" A vein on her forehead throbbed. Her neck was taut, the skin stretched along the sides into a couple of knife edges. A red flush swept across her cheeks up to her hairline.

He'd only imagined she could get that mad. For a second, he flashed on what it must have been like for Cam's husband that time they'd had their little marital chat.

"Look, don't be angry," he said. "We need more information before we can do anything. How do we know they're not playing bingo in there or if it's just some other non-legitimate but typical frolicking going on in there?"

"Don't you dare try to trivialize this!" Her voice reached screaming level, which was heightened by having the windows up. "You're a mere amateur now that you're retired, and whoever you sent in there probably is too. You have no business—"

She might have raged on but got interrupted by three black SUVs pulling up. Al saw a couple more swing around to the back of the building. Cam's mouth clicked shut. She stared at the vans but not with anything close to surprise.

Al's mouth was hanging open, he realized, as men in black with a bold white *FBI* on each flak jacket tumbled out of the vans and stormed toward the building. The tactical team had a tight seal on the place. Maury was in there. Fergie had ducked down low in Al's truck, but the team was experienced enough to sweep the cars in the lot, and Al watched two of the men in black tug Fergie out and spread her against the side of Al's truck. *She can't be enjoying that.*

He glanced toward Cam. A small smile was trying to tug its way onto that Sphinx of a face of hers. The men in black sure were efficient. They popped the building's front door and soon were lining up a group of young women and a separate group of men outside.

Al didn't take long to spot the control central of the storm. A woman in the same black gear, with two of the biggest men on the tactical team on either side of her, left the last vehicle and walked across to where the men and women had been clustered into groups. Fergie stood among the women now, towering above the others, most of whom were barely over five feet tall.

Al opened his door and started out the door.

"Stay here!" Cam shouted.

He glared at her, got out of her car, and started across to the parking lot.

"You'll just mess things up!" she shouted.

Al didn't slow but walked faster.

He held up his wallet badge high to the first of the men to spot him and pivot to point their weapons his way. He didn't slow, though two of them stepped to block his path to the woman. He walked up to them and shouted around them.

"Danielle!"

She turned her head, saw him, and yelled, "Let him through."

He knew her. Danielle Cassidy, an FBI special agent out of Houston, was heading up the FBI's end of the push against human trafficking.

She turned back to watch the men in black bring out the last few stragglers from inside. Her long black hair hung down over the back of her flak jacket, her skin pale porcelain, nose chiseled thin, with the intensity of a hawk three inches from a running mouse, talons extended and plummeting to earth far faster than the mouse was going.

"Two of these people are mine," Al said. "I just sent one inside. The other was in the parking lot."

"Let me guess," Danielle said without turning toward him, "the redheaded Amazon in with the women. You're going to have to point the man out. They all look like they were caught with a hand in the cookie jar to me."

Al pointed out Maury, who looked agitated, mostly because he got stopped before anything really entertaining could happen inside.

"You're a long way from home, Danielle," Al said.

She nodded, staying focused on her team in action.

Fergie and Maury were ushered over to where Al stood with Danielle.

"I showed your men my badge," Fergie said. "Retired city PD detective."

"I know. Rule one is round everyone up, sort later."

Whatever Fergie was going to say, which Al gathered from Fergie's expression was going to put a bee in Danielle's ear, got stepped on by Cam, who held her shield high and shouted as she came nearer, "He's not bothering you, is he?"

Danielle leaned closer to Al. "She doesn't mean you, does she?"

"New partner," he said back to her in a soft voice. "She's still breaking me in."

"Well, good luck to her on that," Danielle said.

The two men who dropped Maury off spun and went back to their other tasks as soon as Danielle gave them a dismissive sign.

"Danielle, this is Maury, my brother," Al said.

"Really?" Danielle held out a hand. She shook Fergie's hand too when she stepped in closer.

"You sent your brother into a place like this?" Cam's voice was still an octave above normal.

"Got yanked out all too soon," Maury muttered.

"I was trying to find out what we now know in a less subtle way." Al waved a hand toward the group of women. "Do you notice anything obvious?"

"Hey, they're all Asian," Danielle said. "I thought the bones were from a mix of races."

"What bones?" Al asked, looking at Cam. "We didn't send out any report about bones."

"They could still be trafficked women," Cam said.

"Could be? They'd damn well better be," Danielle said. "I can't bring a strike team in on a hunch."

Before the delightful turn of conversation could go any further, Al's cell phone rang. He took it out. Bonnie was calling. He'd told her not to call unless there was an emergency.

He stepped away from the others and answered. "What is it?"

Seconds later, he snapped the phone shut. "Maury. Fergie. Let's go. Someone tried to break into the house."

"Is Bonnie hurt?" Fergie asked.

"No, but Tanner is. Bonnie's with him at the vet."

He spun and took off running toward his truck. Maury and Fergie ran right at his heels.

"Is he hurt bad?" Maury yelled.

"I don't know! I don't know!" Now Al's voice was up an octave.

"Hey, are you just going to take off and leave me?" Cam shouted.

He didn't look back or slow but just kept running as hard as he could.

CHAPTER ELEVEN

THE LIGHTS FROM THE TRUCK's dash gave Al's anguished face a greenish-blue hue. Fergie watched him accelerate into the turns and push up the hills, all within the speed limits but barely so. She'd never figured him for a sentimental person and had wondered if he was capable of loving ever again, of feeling even deep affection. She and everyone else knew about that business with Abbie and Maury, how he'd kept to himself since, his insides scarred and insensitive as far as she had ever seen. Still, she felt a mix of sympathy and something more for him, maybe a feather of hope that he could open up to care about things again, first dogs, perhaps people next— people like her.

In low, tired whispers, they had talked in the night, waiting for the sweat on their bodies to dry, her head resting in the crook of his arm. In the daytime, he could be about as chatty as a deep-water clam. But when he was—call it *relaxed*—she had leaped at the chance to hear him express himself. "What is it you thought you'd be doing with your life?"

"Not this," he said.

"How did you picture your days?"

"Fishing. Reading. Music, chess, the usual exercise, and getting around."

"By yourself?"

"That's how it was shaping up until all of you were foisted off on me."

"Oh, and now we're a burden?"

"Well, maybe not as much as I'd thought. Just different from what I had pictured."

"Am I a bad thing?"

"Well, yes..." He gave the pause two full beats. "But in a good way."

She'd shoved at him and felt something that made her draw her hand back. "Oh my gosh. You're ready to go again."

"I said different, not dead."

At the present moment, as he drove through the darkening grip of night, a vein in Al's neck bulged and throbbed, and his hands were talons gripping the wheel, claws that grew whiter as he squeezed.

"Al?" Maury said.

Al didn't glance to the backseat where Maury sat.

Fergie took a long, slow, deep breath and reached to hold the handle above the window on the passenger side as Al took a sharp turn. The other side of all that was inside Al could be a volcano. She and Maury and Bonnie had seen it. He wasn't a huge man, five eleven to her six two, and when she wore heels, forget about it. But she'd seen him snap a guy's neck like it was a small stick pretzel, his jaws clenched and anger shooting out of his eyes in livid sparks. He'd had some kind of military hand-to-hand training way back—some he talked about, some he didn't. It and his anger, as well as an uncanny speed for a guy his age, had tipped the balance several times. It had saved all of their lives. However, it was nothing to mess with, and from the look of his jaw, it was very near the surface again.

Both his hands stayed clenched on the wheel. He

had firm grasping arms, ones that could caress when they wanted. His lips pressed in a tight line as he stared straight ahead. *Those lips.* The biggest surprise about him had come in bed, as surprises sometimes do. He'd opened a gate of himself that was pure, unbridled passion. It had jolted her the first time and, of course, pleased her. Later, she thought of that pure, stark emotion when he was fighting—wide open, furious, and no holds barred. That didn't bode well at present. She was seeing that swinging door he'd once talked about, only the dark, hard-edged side of it. His lack of expression was just the volcano perking up. If something bad had happened to Tanner, someone—whoever had done it—was in for a world of hurt.

He liked classical music when he listened to the radio at all, and she nearly reached to turn on the radio but figured even it wouldn't calm the savage beast at that particular moment. She glanced into the backseat, where Maury rode with wide eyes and mouth pressed shut. He knew.

Al turned the truck into the vet's gravel lot and swung into a parking spot with a small spray of stones. He shot out of the door, left it open with the keys still in the ignition, and dashed toward the front door.

"I've seen him like this before," Maury said.

"Never pretty, is it?" Fergie asked.

"I just hope nothing is so wrong that Tanner dies."

By the time Fergie got inside and spotted Bonnie standing next to what must be the vet, Al was hunched over the table where Tanner lay on his side. Tanner's eyes were closed.

Please don't let him be dead. Fergie rushed forward. She pressed against Al's rigid side, leaned close enough to the table to see Tanner's chest lifting and falling. *Whew.* He was breathing.

Bandages crisscrossed Tanner's chest. White tape covered the end of one ear, and his left front leg was wrapped in a blue cast.

"Had to sedate him to set the leg," the vet said. "He'll favor it but can get around on it if he needs to. Cracked ribs will keep him sore a while, too. Little fella's lucky to be alive. Someone kicked him good." She was a solid woman in her fifties, with a white gown, graying hair, and a serious look she probably wore more than she liked. The laugh lines around her mouth and eyes said she had a sense of humor, though she didn't get to use it at the moment. "This was definitely beyond an urgent-care-status case."

Al looked at her and tilted his head.

She explained. "Urgent-care situations are pet conditions that are not life-threatening to the animal but need to be addressed before the next available appointment." The vet reached down to smooth a roughed patch of Tanner's fur. "That's when we work to get the animal seen in between other scheduled appointments. *This* was an emergency. I'm glad the young lady brought him in when she did."

Fergie figured the emergency status would be reflected in the vet's billing. Any cost issues went right past Al. His thoughts seemed to be on something else.

Al glanced toward Bonnie.

"I was downstairs doing a load of wash and heard something. Someone was in the house. He was barking like all get out. Time I got upstairs and fetched your Sig Sauer out of the gun safe, the truck was pulling out. Tanner was hurt. He'd been defending the house. Like the doc says, someone kicked him. Hard. More than once. I had to get him right here."

"Blue truck? Red driver's-side door?"

"Yeah. How did you know?" Bonnie cocked her head at Al.

"Is Tanner going to be all right?" Al asked the vet.

"Jury's still out about any internal injuries. But he tests out okay for now. It'll be a few days before he's feeling anything like chipper. He's a tough little scamp, though, and I think he's gonna be fine, though I'd keep a close eye on him. He sure must've put up a pretty good fight."

"Okay. Thanks, Doc. Call a cab, you guys." Al spun and ran toward the door.

"Why?" Fergie yelled.

"So you can get home."

Fergie raced after him. By the time she got out the front door, he was already in his truck, the door slammed, and was pulling out of the parking lot. She didn't even try to run after him, unable to have caught him even if she had a jet pack. He was off and away with squealing tires.

Bonnie and Maury pushed out the door to stand beside Fergie.

"Oh, my. My. My. My," Bonnie said.

Maury shook his head.

Fergie dug in her pocket and got out her cell phone. "I hate to do this, but better we don't have to visit Al in the big house." She punched in Clayton's number.

———⬦———

Al didn't push the speed limits but drove in a straight and deliberate way to the trailer court where Toby Buchanan's dad had lived, where Toby did live.

He went over and over the scene in his mind: the burglar pushing through the doorway after breaking the door; little Tanner barking, taking a stand; the kick, maybe multiple kicks until Tanner flew across the room. Al had to let up on his grip on the steering wheel. It felt as if he were going to tear it in half.

He pulled into the trailer court, one he'd been in too many times before, twice to close down a meth lab. His lights swept across the ends of trailers in a row. That was no place the gentry lived. During a daytime visit once, he'd seen a woman in a dirty pink sweat suit hanging out clothes on a line stretched from her trailer to a light post. An older man had sat in the shade of his awning beside a table that had once been an electric-company spool. Every time Al came through, he tried to clear his mind of every cliché the place encouraged, but it lived up to them each time, from pit bulls to shirtless young men tinkering under the open hoods of aging cars and trucks.

Al eased up to the trailer on the end, the blue truck with the red door in front, though his temptation was to arrive in a spray of gravel. He got out of his truck and locked the door. He let his Glock stay inside the glove box, not trusting the rage bubbling and boiling his blood while surging through every vein. Outside the trailer door, he took ten long breaths, in and out, in and out, then knocked.

He heard movement inside, but no one came to the door.

The storm door had no glass or screen, but he had to swing it open and hold it with his left hand and kick at the door just beside the lock and knob. After two kicks, the door swung inward, more announcement than he would have liked.

He saw movement to his left. Toby scurried away from him down a hallway past a breakfast nook and a door that opened to the bathroom. At the end of the hall were rumpled sheets on a king-size bed. Toby stopped once inside the bedroom door and turned to look at Al, who caught something in his expression. His eyes seemed to focus just over Al's left shoulder. Al dropped to the floor, letting his weight pull him down like one of those wooden toys where you press on the bottom, loosening strings to make the figure collapse. Al collapsed.

A bat whooshed head high through the space where he'd been standing and smashed against the wooden paneling of the wall beside the door, leaving a deep, bat-shaped hole in the wall. Al twisted to look up and saw Donnie Farris. Al hadn't met him, though he'd seen a photo of him in the Farris home.

Donnie pulled the bat back to smash down at Al where he lay on the floor. Al raised himself on his hands to kick upward as hard as he could before Donnie could swing downward. Donnie jumped back just before the kick connected. He rushed back toward Al with the bat poised for a crushing swing.

Al glanced next to where he lay on the far-from-clean carpet. A television sat just inside the door—his television. Parts of his stereo were next to that, along with a half dozen two-foot lengths of what looked like tubing. It wasn't much, but Al grabbed one. It was heavier than he expected, more like a meaty baton than a tube. Donnie swung the bat down at Al, who rolled out of the way. Al snapped the end of the baton up and caught Donnie in the desired target that time. By the time Donnie registered the baton heading for his crotch, it had landed and landed hard.

Donnie's eyes slammed shut. Al heard Toby's pounding steps as he ran toward Al to help Donnie. Al sprang up and punched Donnie as hard as he could in the stomach. He spun just in time for Toby to get all the way to him. Al dropped the baton—*too hefty; he'd kill the little fuck.* He let his own swinging momentum keep him going. He brought up an elbow and forearm and caught Toby across the jaw, sending him across the open living area to flip over a couch.

Al started to step around Donnie to go after Toby, when he heard a yell from the open door. "Stay right where you are, and get those hands up high!"

He spun and saw Cam. She had her service piece out and leveled right at his chest.

"What the hell are you doing?" he asked.

He looked down at the heavy baton he'd dropped earlier to thump on the carpet. The center was inch-thick copper. Toby was lucky Al hadn't used that on him.

"Clayton sent me to make sure you didn't do anything stupid, and I was almost in time."

"Put the gun down."

"No." She maintained her stance.

"Are you kidding me?"

"Look, Al. I checked your record at the department, going back to your military record. You have a silver star, for God's sake. You've had extensive training in hand-to-hand combat. That works in your favor as a law officer. It'll go against you if you kill this bit of toe jam. Don't make me have to do something stupid on top of what you've done."

"It would be stupid, all right."

"As much as I would have no personal issue with you throwing these two scum buckets around like hacky sacks, I'm here as a deputy of the law, and... like it or not, so are you. Turn around."

"You're going to cuff me?"

"Have to until I sort this out."

"But one of these assholes kicked my dog while they were breaking into my house."

"That's what you say, but we have no proof of that.

THROW THE TEXAS DOG A BONE

Turn around. I mean it." She waved the barrel of her gun at him.

He did so slowly. If she wanted to push it, she had him for B and E as well as assault. He felt his inner heat rising again as she clicked on the cuffs.

"At least take a glance at that bat. And that thick wire."

She picked up the bat and looked at the end. "Yep. It's one of the ones stolen from the school. Shame I can't take it with us." She looked at the heavy stretch of wire with its inch-thick copper. "Don't know what this is."

"It's hard evidence."

"Tainted. You know that. Come busting in here without a warrant..."

Toby pushed himself up from the other side of his sofa. He picked up on what was going on, and his eyes widened. "Ha," he said, but as he did, two or three teeth fell out of his mouth. He was reaching to catch them as Cam turned Al and headed him toward the door out of the trailer.

Donnie was stirring from where he was stretched out on the stained carpet. "Oughta sue," he mumbled.

Al nodded toward his television set and part of his stereo system resting on the floor just inside the door, all they'd had time to grab.

"Those are from my house," Al said, "It was burgled today. That would be hard evidence."

"Not gathered the way you got in here," Cam said.

She pushed him outside, which even late in the day seemed a whole lot brighter than he remembered. Heat was rising in wavy ripples from the squad car. She opened the back door and pushed down on his head as she eased him into the backseat so he wouldn't bonk his head getting in. He glanced toward the trailer. Donnie and Toby came out onto the steps to watch Al get hauled away. Both were grinning, though Toby's smile looked more like a broken picket fence.

Uriah Voltag put down his binoculars and rolled up his window. He waited until he'd started the minivan before clicking on his hands-free cell phone.

"Yes?" The tinny voice always sounded a little outer spacey to him, but he couldn't deny the tone, which always sat right on the edge of irritation.

"The feds are packing up and leaving, but it looks like that's it for the Red Barn for a while."

"Did you call and warn them in time?"

"I called... but not in time." Uriah glanced in the rearview mirror. *No tail.*

"That wasn't the best place for us, anyway. Too young. You know what I need, and you know the other places to check."

The phone clicked off.

Should have gone to college. Well, no hope for that at the moment.

He turned left at the next light. *Yeah, I know where to go.*

He rolled down his window and kept it open, even with the air conditioning on. No matter what he'd done, he hadn't been able get the last of that odor out. *Can't just take it to have it detailed.* He sighed and rolled the window down some more despite how hot it was outside.

The deputy outside the conference room, Pudge Simmons, kept as straight a face as he could manage and gestured for Al and Cam to go on in. Al opened the door, held it for Cam, and followed her in.

Al rubbed his wrists and didn't once glance in Cam's direction.

The first person to catch Al's eye as he entered the room was Danielle Cassidy, the FBI special agent out of Houston, heading up the FBI's end of the push against human trafficking. She sat at one end of the table. Clayton rose from the seat next to her.

"I hear she brought you in wearing cuffs," Clayton said to Al.

"It hasn't been an altogether pleasant day up to now. Can we get on with what we're here about?"

"We can talk about charges after a bit," Cam said.

"There aren't going to be any charges," Clayton said. "We can always say 'probable cause.' What we have to worry about is that little snot suing us. I've put a pair of detectives on counter initiative. They're headed out there with a proper warrant this time—what Al should have done in the first place, had he not been under personal duress. I'll also have one of them drive Al's truck back here."

"Personal duress?" Cam asked.

Clayton stayed fixed on Al. "You did say you saw some of your burgled stuff out there, didn't you, Al?"

"And evidence on the concrete-plant jobs too."

"Do tell."

"Three concrete plants in different parts of Travis County got hit: boom, boom, boom—Alamo Concrete, Lauren Concrete, and TXI Concrete. The MO was the same in each, with the perps breaking into a gate and heading straight toward the underground wiring, where they used some sort of vehicle to winch up the wiring. At the TXI facility on Harold Green Road, they stole close to one thousand feet of copper wiring, but not just any wiring. The copper wiring used in concrete plants for electrical purposes is about an inch thick. One foot of the copper wiring is believed to weigh about a pound, that's with copper reselling at three fifty per pound. It's lucky they didn't electrocute themselves in the process, but they were just clever enough and dumb-lucky to pull it off. What I saw in the trailer were two-foot-long sample lengths of that wire that could come from only one place."

"Let's hope they didn't think to clear all the evidence out of there by the time my guys arrive," Clayton said.

Danielle cleared her throat.

"Okay," Clayton said, "go ahead and get it off your chest."

"I don't know if the three of you are aware of this, but the city police chief fired one of their detectives today, a Dennis Cranston." She looked around at each of them.

Al knew Dennis. Guy thought he was Charlie Siringo, cowboy detective. He dressed the part and walked as though he'd just gotten off a horse. He also combed his hair with some sort of greasy Tiger Balm, talked loudly when in a group, and drank hard with his colleagues off duty. Al didn't care for him and knew Fergie had declined to be his partner back when she was a city detective.

"He was let go for a variety of policy violations—improper burglary investigations, dishonesty, improperly handling and documenting evidence, excessive use of force, failure to follow up with witnesses, and a number of other charges. It was a really long list. I'm surprised he was tolerated as long as he was." Danielle looked around the table to each of them.

"I knew the guy," Al said. He wondered why she'd brought up his name. Al had first heard of the guy when he'd made something of a splash in a southeast Austin so-called race riot. That was when Dennis was still in uniform, before he became a detective. A mixed crowd of blacks and a few Latinos had been kicking up a fuss outside a nightspot at almost 3:00 a.m., spoiling for a fight perhaps, but hardly a riot. But that was the way Dennis called it in to dispatch. He must have read somewhere about those early Texas Rangers who liked to say, "One riot, one Ranger."

He'd driven straight toward the crowd at speed, slammed on the brakes to slide sideways toward them. When the squad car had stopped in a squeal of tires and spray of loose gravel he'd grabbed the shotgun from its rest, hopped out, and fired twice into the air. The crowd dispersed in all directions. A minute or two later, the parking lot beside the club was empty. He picked up his radio mic, called in, and asked, "What riot?" forgetting cleverly that he was the one who'd called it in as a riot. His supervising officer hadn't been pleased. That was just one of many bumps on the slow upward path that eventually led to Dennis becoming a detective and getting to dress like Will Rogers on steroids whenever he could.

He glanced toward Cam. "What's your point?"

"At the Bureau, we play by far higher standards and for far higher stakes. A person like that wouldn't have been hired, much less tolerated to the extent he was. But this is the maverick nature of detectives at the local level." She nodded.

"Since I'm not the one who called you and your tactical team in on this, how is it germane, Danielle?" Clayton's voice had dropped to a low rumble.

"The tip we got, that the Red Barn was a human-trafficking lead, was a bust." She was looking at Cam. "They were running some gals, but they all had papers, and what they were doing was illegal, but it's nothing that belonged on my plate. Waste of my frigging time, if you ask me, and taxpayer dollars." She stood up.

"I'll... I'll look into any other leads, see if they aren't more up your alley," Cam said.

"You're going to be riding patrol again for the rest of the week," Clayton said.

"Where?"

"Oh, some of the outlying areas."

Al knew that would mean some of the roughest trouble spots in the county. "What about me?" he asked.

"Your dog's hurt, right? You should take some time. Tend to him."

"Fine with me," Al said.

Going out, he got to the door before Cam, but she went on through with stiff, brisk strides and didn't look back once as she stormed off down the hall.

A dozen steps down the hall, she turned her head to yell back over her shoulder at Al, "This is all your stupid fault!"

CHAPTER TWELVE

TANNER LAY CURLED ON THE end of Al's bed. Al, Maury, Bonnie, and Fergie were all hovering around. The dog looked up at them with tired eyes he struggled to keep open. Al thought the little guy looked happy to be home, though. Al was petting Tanner's head and getting licks in return. Bonnie sat on the bed, smoothing Tanner's fur.

"You turned out to be a heck of a watchdog," Al said. "I'm just sorry I wasn't able to do more than I did to those who hurt you."

"And you're still out a television and stereo," Maury said. "Well, we're out. There are a couple of shows I'm going to miss, but I suppose I'll manage somehow." He gave Bonnie a quick glance.

"From what I hear, the deputies found nothing at the trailer, and the guys are hiring themselves a lawyer to sue the sheriff," Fergie said.

"They're hiring Bobby Briscoe, that TV ambulance-chasing lawyer, who only gets called because his commercial shows dozens of times a day. His phone number is just one numeral repeated, and he claims he gets his clients 'hunnerts' of dollars. His catch phrase is a hard snap of his fingers while saying, 'It's as easy as snap.' Good luck to him. Clayton's law team will tear him to shreds and rip him a new asshole in the process," Al said.

"Don't forget that you're out of a job," Maury said.

"One I wasn't getting paid to do and was just doing as a courtesy. One that had been turned into a pain in the behind by Cam 'Brickhead' Callaghan."

"Maybe she's not as bad as you think," Bonnie said.

"She took me in at gunpoint and made me wear handcuffs and ride in the back of the cruiser. The guys are still making jokes about it."

"Well, hell, Al, I've wished I could get you into cuffs a few times myself." Bonnie grinned.

"Maybe you can help Fergie with the case she's working on," Maury said.

"Okay with me," Fergie said.

Al looked up into her eyes.

Fergie winked slowly and held a finger up to her lips.

For a second, Al read that the wrong way until she pointed down at the dog. He had thought for a moment she was hushing him about some of the antics they'd been up to on that same bed, antics that had made him feel about seventeen again inside.

He looked down at the bed. Tanner's eyes had drooped then shut all the way in spite of all his efforts to keep them open and savor the moment. Al and the others eased away from the bed and left the room. Bonnie was the last one out. She closed the door quietly behind them, leaving Tanner to his healing rest.

<hr>

Night settled in slowly and uncomfortably. Al felt a restless itch as he glanced from inside at the mirror of darkened windows facing the lake and running along the kitchen to his right, past the dining area in the middle, to the edge of the living room, an open area of the top floor that took a dogleg into that space that was missing a television and stereo. Maury and Bonnie plopped into chairs at the dining table while Fergie went to the fridge and held up four long-necked bottles of Dos Equis. Maury and Bonnie both nodded.

Al shook his head. He went to the counter and measured out coffee beans into the grinder. Above its gnashing whir, Fergie opened three of the beers and took them to the table and sat, sliding two of them to Maury and Bonnie. They all watched Al.

He poured the ground coffee into a filter he tucked inside a Melitta ceramic cone. Al favored the drip method, pouring heated water over the coffee to let it trickle down into a thermos. He filled the teapot with fresh water and put it on the range at medium high.

He paused to listen for a moment to the wind rubbing against the house, limbs of one live oak scratching gently while the breeze coming across the water pushed, massaged, and nudged against the house. One or two boards creaked in his home, where he'd expected to spend a great deal of time alone. If his pals had told him he'd been establishing a nest, he might have denied it. If they had told him it would be peopled with as many persons as lived it in right then, he'd have called them outright liars.

"You didn't seem all that upset that the deputies Clayton sent to Toby's trailer came away empty handed," Fergie said.

"I expected it."

"Did you, now?"

"That the deputies found nothing is a good thing. It means the merch, which includes my TV and stereo, is on the move. Maybe we can make something come of that."

"How?"

"Do you recall our acquaintance Irving Dagrell, the

owner of Rudy's Railyard, that pawn-and-military-paraphernalia shop?"

"Ah, yes. How could I forget? Slimy little man." Fergie's lip curled for a moment, and not in an attractive, Elvis sort of way. "No priors. But he likes to fly to Mexico, the Philippines, and Bangkok, where he can be with eleven – and twelve-year-old girls. Brags about it to his men friends because, as he says, 'it's practically legal in those places.' Clean as a whistle in the States. Just meeting the guy made my skin crawl."

"That's the guy," Al said. "I keep hoping with someone like him that he turns out to be more complex than he seems, that maybe he's keeping a charity afloat somewhere or helping a senior citizen live better final days. But no soap. Scratch beneath the surface, and you get the same old Irving. Want to see if we can kick a little dirt in his eyes and see how he squeals?"

Fergie nodded. "Let's go. I think it's time karma loaded up a fist filled with a roll of nickels in it for that guy. I'd be glad to be a part of that."

"Good. Aside from being a clear foot taller than him, I think you scare him on general principle. You're the opposite of what he likes: petite, vulnerable women." Al could have added "young," but his wiser side prevailed.

"No one calls me petite," Bonnie said, "though I'm short."

"You're a muffin," Maury said. "But one that packs a mean left... and right, not to mention being a crack shot."

"I take it you're not done with those cases you were working on for Clayton." Bonnie tilted her head up at Al.

"I can't believe you know Al and have to ask," Maury said. "He's always been part bulldog. You remember that blue-boat incident? Al was eight years before he wrapped that up, but he never let it go of it. I think Clayton is just trying to fire Al up more by ordering him to the sidelines while there are two unfinished cases he was working on, one of them now involving the burglary of this house."

Al caught himself grinding his teeth and made himself stop. He turned up the heat on the burner half a tick. The pot made noise as the water bubbled.

"Maybe while you and I try to clean up what you left unfinished on your plate, you can help me with what I'm working on," Fergie said.

"What do you have in mind?"

"Maybe on our way to rattle Irving's pathetic cage, we can have a look at this doctor's place. I could use fresh eyes and a new perspective. Doug Chandle is off looking into the guy's background at the Houston hospital where he worked last. I can't get over how the doc looks on the up-and-up to me. Perhaps you can convince me this isn't some kind of witch hunt, one that doesn't make sense for this hospital, if you ask me."

"Hospitals are super risk cautious these days."

"I know that. Still." Fergie took a sip of her beer.

Al poured hot water over the coffee grounds. He put the pot back on the range, where it started to whistle until he turned the heat back to medium low. "Did you look at the guy's finances?"

"Looked to be pretty straightforward to me. No offshore accounts on the Cayman Islands or anything like that, at least as far as I could find."

"I'd like to see where the guy lives."

"Fine. You can drive." Fergie held up her beer.

"Can you two keep an eye on Tanner until we get back?" Al asked.

Maury gave Bonnie a look, which she returned, each masking a sly smile.

"Sure," Bonnie said. "Sure thing."

"Yeah. No worries, Al," Maury said.

Al finished making the coffee and picked up the thermos and a couple of mugs.

"Ready?" he asked Fergie.

Fergie gulped down the last of her beer and followed Al out to his truck.

He got in, and as she strapped herself in, he turned to her. "Am I seeing what I think I am?"

"About what?"

"About Maury and Bonnie."

"Probably."

"When did this start up? I thought she wouldn't have anything to do with him."

"He's changing. Not all at once, but gradually. She's feeling kinder about him. We have a theory, she and I. We think it comes from being around you."

"Well, if push comes to shove, I'm betting he's still a horndog at heart."

"But in a good way."

"There's a good way?"

"Bonnie says he's got a lot of energy now that he's recovered, and she speculates that he's bound to have some skills."

"Skills?"

"You can't be a womanizer most of your life without acquiring skills."

"Well, I just hope Bonnie isn't settling. And I mean that in a way that has nothing to do with me."

"That's your brother you're talking about."

"I know. I love my brother, but I don't know if he's capable of change, however much we might desire it. I guess she'll find out, one way or the other."

———◆———

Al pulled his truck over to the curb, where he and Fergie

could look up a steeply sloping lawn to a three-story yellow stone house. Landscaping lights pointed at key trees and hedges lit up the sides of the house, letting them see all they needed to at that hour.

He turned the engine off and poured two mugs of coffee. They sat there for a moment, staring up at the house. "Who is this guy again?"

"A surgeon. Dr. August Rose Corneille," she said. "Doug says his colleagues and golfing pals call him Bud, a nickname from his childhood the doctor claims came not from the usual 'bud' as a friend but because he wasn't a fully blooming rose yet. More likely, it was a boyhood twist on 'Rosebud.'"

"You mean the sled in Citizen Kane?"

"No. You know. Just 'rosebud.' The flower. Maybe he was a late bloomer. Some people are."

Al's head turned toward her. "And maybe all that was made up to make him seem more human."

"That could be as well."

"You've been in the doctor's office?" Al asked.

"Yes. Just enough for a quick look-around. Not while he was there, of course. I haven't met the man in person. Doug has. I've been doing the usual double-dipping of all the background checks. I found nothing. Everything squeaked, it was so clean."

"What did the office look like when you were making your unofficial visit?"

"Like he went to an interior designer and said, 'Make it look like an office.'"

"But nothing personal or even distinctive, right?" he said.

"Nope."

"Now, take a look at his landscaping."

"Same thing. Looks like he ordered it put in but didn't

care enough to personalize it in any way. Could just be he's married to his work, dedicated. Everything else just needs to be kept so-so nice by hired help."

Al shook his head. "That's the impression I got. How long did Doug say he'd worked at that other hospital in Houston?"

"Seven years."

"And before that?"

"Six in Atlanta. A brief stint in Orlando before that."

"For a very good surgeon, he's been a real jumping bean, hasn't he?"

"And? What am I to make of that?"

"Maybe nothing. It's something to puzzle over. You say he seems a nice-enough person, one who's doing good things. Right?"

"Yes. I don't know, Al. I might like the guy if I met him. He strikes me as a misunderstood do-gooder."

"But your perception of him being 'nice' could be superficial, a bit like the landscaping, a calculated and orchestrated effect. The hospital, after all, is curious about him but won't say why, won't tell you what makes them edgy."

"Right."

"Well, something's there, or the hospital is throwing good money out its window, which doesn't seem to be a standard practice for them. They usually seem more preoccupied with raking the green stuff in. About the only thing I know could make them as nervous as a long-tailed cat in a room full of rocking chairs is something that might impugn their integrity, enough to lead to a lawsuit. You haven't turned up anything like that?"

"Not so far."

"Okay, then. Now, what say we hit my agenda item for the night?"

He gulped down the rest of his cup, opened his window to shake out the last few drops, and started the truck.

———————◆◇◆———————

Al drove to a storage-unit facility whose front gate was open in spite of the late hour. That made the place attractive to some. The back was fenced and sealed off, but renters could come and go at all hours. He pulled into the lot and eased his truck to the far back, where it could be as out of sight as possible yet give them a view of the row he wanted and anyone coming in late.

Mounted lights at the corners of buildings lit the rows enough so anyone could get to and find their storage unit at night.

Al turned off the engine and reached for the thermos to pour more coffee.

"Gosh, it's been ages since I was out parking." Fergie took the warm mug he held out to her.

"You probably enjoy a stakeout more than Cam did. We were barely getting an early picture on the Red Barn when Danielle and her tactical team swooped in."

"You really think Cam's the one who tipped them off?"

"I don't know anything for absolute sure. But I do know that to muster and roll with that many people all the way from Houston, for what had to be a half-baked scrap of information at that point, smacks of desperation on someone's part. Maybe Danielle hasn't made a recent flashy bust in Houston."

"Don't they have a fair bit of human trafficking over there?"

"It's one of the biggest centers in America—port city like that, centrally located, a lot of transient workers coming and going, hitting the port like sailors on leave. You bet. Years ago, they used to recruit the gals from the Pacific

Rim, Russia, Central and South America and fly them in with the usual quick passports, promising the women jobs in restaurants. The promised life always sounded better than the abusive, dysfunctional, or just plain crowded places where the girls lived. When the airports tightened, the handlers found other ways to bring them in. Wide-eyed young women—and some young men—eager for new lives came trickling through in hordes, all facing a bubble that was about to pop hard."

"You know, I ran into plenty of the same as a city detective." Fergie took a sip of coffee and looked at Al over the rim. "But the FBI rushing over before doing a lot of preliminary checking first, that's new to me. I never got blindsided like that before."

"Yeah, unless they had done some preliminary checking, and we were the ones starting to crowd *their* bust. Turned out to be a bust of a bust at that, though."

"I imagine that gives Cam something to think about while she's riding around patrolling the far, rough extremes of the county."

"Quite different from us sitting out here in the middle of Bumfart, Nowhere waiting for the likes of Irving."

"Why do you think, out of all the pawnshop dealers in this area, that Irving holds promise for you?"

"It's a hunch. If I was someone the likes of Toby, who needed a quick fence, I'd think of Irving. He has a rep, and his pawnshop's not far from the garage where Toby worked. Irving's also had dealings in the past with scrap metal, which makes him attractive if you happen to have a thousand pounds of copper. Each foot weighs a pound and is worth about three-fifty. Cut into two-foot lengths for storage and handling, it's still a half a ton of copper worth about thirty-five hundred. That's not big-time crime, but it's still a felony, as is fencing it for them."

"Hasn't someone checked Irving's store?"

"Several times. I'd like to say I used the same trick I suggested to Cam of taking Irving's picture around to storage-unit facilities, and that this one rang the gong. But, in fact, I followed him out here once from the back of his store."

"And here I thought you'd used that powerful brain of yours to deduce all this."

"Hey, shhh. This might be him."

A white panel van pulled off the highway into the storage facility, lit brightly at first by the spotlights at the front, then showing more dimly as the van moved slowly up the center of the rows, turning at last into the row Al had been watching. He and Fergie slumped low in their seats. If anyone looked their way, the truck would appear empty and parked for storage.

The driver got out, profiling himself against the white side of the van. *Short enough.* The light caught the face. *Yep, Irving.* Al reached over, popped open the glove box, and took out the Glock. Fergie's long red hair hung like a soft waterfall. The back of his hand brushed against it.

He jacked a shell into the chamber. Fergie whispered, "What about me? No gun?"

"Just seeing all six foot two of you might give the little fucker a heart attack."

"Thanks. Good to know I can still charm the men."

Al turned his dome light off. He eased his door open as soon as Irving rattled the storage unit's door open. Al left his own door open to avoid the noise of closing it. Fergie slipped out her side.

Irving came out and headed to the back of the van. As soon as Fergie came around to the front of his truck, Al motioned her toward one side of the van, and he eased around the other side.

Al came around from the left, and Irving's back was to him. His hands were full. Fergie stepped around from the other side.

"Hey, you little turd!" she yelled. "Where are you going with that?"

Irving's head snapped up. He wore a dark-blue polo shirt over black jeans, an outfit that only made his pale, narrow face look more like that of a startled rodent. His hair was thinning—only a few wisps of hair remained in the tonsure that was shaping up, and Irving often rubbed hard at those hairs, something he couldn't do presently since his hands were full. He let go of what he was carrying and spun to run. However, his eyes opened wide, and he stopped where he stood when he saw Al's gun leveled at him.

"I sure hope that wasn't my TV you just dropped, Irv." Al stepped closer and looked down. "Well, crap. It was."

CHAPTER THIRTEEN

MINUTES AFTER THE SHERIFF'S-DEPARTMENT CRUISER arrived—and Al had been glad to see Cam wasn't in it—he recognized the next vehicle that pulled up. Sheriff Clayton himself stepped out of the driver's side. He wore jeans, boots, and a hunter-green long-sleeved shirt.

"You didn't have to come all the way out here yourself," Al said.

"Oh, I like to see how my retired people are getting along in the use of their spare time. I might be retired myself someday." He didn't grin, but his eyes twinkled as they caught the light from the headlights fixed on the open storage-unit door.

"I think we've just recovered all the missing copper wire from those cement places." Al waved a hand toward the inside of the rental storage unit where the lengths of thick wire were stacked. He nodded toward the smashed television on the ground. "That used to be my television, though there's not much left of it. I can identify and speak for the stereo components, though."

"Good for you. Someday, you may get them back when they're no longer needed in the evidence room."

Clayton stepped over to tower over Irving, who sat on the gravel between the feet of two deputies, his legs crossed. His hands were cuffed behind him.

He looked up at Clayton and said one word: "Lawyer."

Now that his eyes weren't open wide, he just looked like someone about to feel the lash of a whip. His head made furtive shifts to the left and right, never looking quite at anyone.

Clayton glanced into the storage unit himself. "Well, it looks like we've indeed found all the missing copper. Al's identified his stuff, including the broken TV. And I see a whole lot of stuff from other burglaries. You sure you don't want to cut a deal while I'm in the mood?"

"Lawyer," Irving said.

Clayton lifted his head to look at the deputies. "Take him to lockup. Now, don't you dare, either one of you, let leak that Mr. Dagrell here has short eyes. You hear?"

"What're you doing? They'll kill me in there!" Irving yelled.

"Would you like to discuss different accommodations?"

"I said I won't deal."

"Okay. Just think about it. It's a long ride there."

"Are you saying I might fall down the stairs or something like that?"

Clayton just shook his head. The deputies lifted Irving to his feet and led him toward the back door of their cruiser.

Al pulled his truck up in front of his house. A ring of eyes glowing in the reflection from his headlights stood waiting. Deer. His deer.

"They still gather around and sometimes lick their lips when you come home." Fergie broke the silence of their ride back.

"Yeah. For all I know, they could very well be saying, 'You know, we don't have to be vegetarians.' Very Alfred Hitchcock."

"You used to feed the deer that come to your house. Now you don't. Why?" Fergie said.

"It was a drought year. They would have starved. This year, there's plenty for them to eat, and it'll be a good acorn year later."

"But they still come around."

"It's about the only parenting I've ever had to do, but it's up to me to know when they can get by on their own and to let them do it."

"Some people in your department thought feeding deer made you look soft."

"But you know otherwise, don't you?"

"Oh, yeah."

"It's a good idea now and then to keep to yourself what you're capable of, in case you ever need to dip into that."

Al reached over and took out the Glock. As he got out of the truck, he tucked it inside his belt.

"You going to take a quick look around?" Fergie asked.

"Don't need to. The deer already told me. It's all clear. If anyone was around, the deer would be as gone as last Easter."

He unlocked the front door. The lights were out inside except a small one in the kitchen that let them thread their way through the living room, past the couch, where Al noted Maury was sleeping, past the dining and kitchen areas, and to his bedroom.

He swung his bedroom door open and turned on the light. Tanner wasn't on the bed. Al looked around and found the dog on the floor beside the bed, where he usually slept. The little fellow had managed, leg in a cast and all, to get down off the bed to the spot where he felt he belonged.

Tanner lifted his head and blinked his eyes at them,

his nose sniffing and twitching as he assured himself it was them.

Al bent down to rub his head.

"I have the feeling that if we'd been Toby and his pal Donnie, Tanner would have been at us tooth and nail," Fergie said.

"I imagine you're right. He's had a taste and a smell, ones he'll never forget."

Al sat on the side of his bed. Tanner moved closer to rest his chin on Al's shoe.

Fergie sat down next to Al. She turned his face with her hand until they were staring at each other, barely three inches apart. "You know, they always said when I was a police detective that women have an intuition about crime that men can never have. But your antennas are up, and you're at full alert. Why? I can hear your insides whirring like a clock in high gear. You'd better spill. It's something about this whole mess, and Clayton knows or senses something too. What the hell's going on?"

Al reached down and rubbed Tanner's head, but the little fellow didn't stir. Some of the pain meds were probably still working away.

"I don't know, for sure. I sense something, and it's big. And, yeah, Clayton's nose is at full point too. But I doubt he has any better idea than I do. But I know what we have to do first thing in the morning. We need to visit my old friend Clive."

"The ME? How's he involved?"

"It's just a starting place. Or a starting-over place. I feel like we've only been skin deep on something that's rumbling."

"Just a gut feeling, huh? But it's got you strung tight as piano wire. You need to relax."

"The one thing I've learned from a career of doing this

is the 'have something hard in hand' before I act. No sense flying off the handle at even a pretty good guess, much less a wispier one like this."

"Yet I've seen you fly off the handle once or twice."

He winced. "And I was sorry after."

"Not as sorry as the other guy."

He tilted his head as he looked at her. "We've just about exhausted all the topics to discuss."

"We could take a shower together and see what comes up."

He carefully lowered Tanner's head off his shoe onto the rug and followed Fergie at what his drill sergeant from long before would have called a double-time quickstep.

Bonnie lay on her back, looking up at the ceiling. She felt quite alone in the basement guest quarters, having just been getting used to having Fergie as a roommate.

She couldn't hear any movement in the house, no squeaking bed rhythmically getting its headboard pounded against the wall. But she had a pretty good idea of what was going on up there. She gave it another few minutes then tossed the covers off, letting the cool basement air sweep across her nude body. She'd slept in just her skin for as long as she could remember.

Her pink terry robe lay across the foot of the bed. She reached for it and tugged it on. At the bottom of the stairs she hesitated. *Was this really such a good idea? Well, what the hell?* She started up the stairs.

Maury had a quilt-patterned comforter pulled over his head as he stretched across the couch. When she nudged him a couple of times, he stirred and turned toward her, his head shrouded in a hood of the blanket. It made him look like the Unabomber. She had the first of several second thoughts. *Not too late to just gracefully back off.*

"What?" He was clearly not at his best when roused.

"I was just wondering..."

"Wondering what?" He sat upright, the blanket fallen down around his waist. At least he was wearing pajamas—in that case, brown with green pheasants across them, maybe an old set of Al's PJs.

"If you'd like to come downstairs where it's warmer."

"It's warmer down there?"

"You know what I mean."

"Oh." He thought about it. "Oh. Oh." His eyes opened wider.

"Well?"

"What about Al?"

"What about him?" She was starting to think it was a bad idea, a really bad idea.

"Is Fergie up here with...?"

"Yes. Look, I'm offering to show you places only a tattooist has seen. Do you want to come downstairs and have sex or not?"

"Want to? I'm almost done."

"Oh, be still, my beating heart!"

But he threw off his covers and followed her as she headed back down the stairs.

Well, at the very least, I'll find out if he learned anything in those years of being a skirt chaser.

CHAPTER FOURTEEN

C LIVE BARNES LOOKED UP FROM his desk in the corner of the morgue when Al and Fergie came in the next morning. His eyes looked rested enough to glitter with excitement again. "Well, you must have ESPN or something."

"I don't even have a television anymore. Didn't have cable or satellite when I did," Al said. "You know Fergie."

Clive and Fergie nodded to each other.

Clive touched a button at the corner of his desk, and a soft *bong* sounded in the lab.

"I'll let her have the honors. She's the one with the discovery, and she is dying to tell you herself."

"Who?" Fergie asked.

"Teddy. His assistant," Al told her.

"When we got the bones back from the anthropologist friend of mine at the campus, she was messing around with them the way she does, putting them into rows, large to small, that sort of thing."

"And?"

"She found something. Ah, here she comes. I'll let her show you."

Teddy came into the room, clutching a broom in one hand. When she turned from closing the door, she looked at Fergie, stiffened, and slowed her steps.

"It's okay." Al stepped closer to Fergie, put an arm

around her shoulders. "It's not the other one. This is my friend Fergie."

Teddy's shoulders relaxed, and her pace picked up, once again eager.

She went right past them and rushed over to a brightly lit steel table where a tray of the bones rested. Clive rose. He and Fergie and Al went over to crowd closer. Teddy gave Al an upward sideways glance and half a grin. She seemed very anxious and proud of herself.

"Show them what you detected, Teddy," Clive said.

Teddy pointed with a trembling finger to scratches on what looked like part of a rib to Al. Then she picked up the biggest piece of skull and held it up to Al. Her eyes flicked to Fergie and seemed reassured when Fergie leaned closer and looked eager.

"What?" Al asked. He glanced to Clive.

"Eye socket."

"Well, I'll be darned." Al reached to take the skull from Teddy. "What would make marks like these?"

"Well, a scalpel might."

"Why would someone be using a scalpel inside an eye socket?" Al stood up straight, the answer coming to him as soon as he'd said it. He looked toward Fergie. She'd gotten it too, in the same instant.

"Well, Teddy, you are an absolute princess," Fergie said. She bent close to look at the skull piece then straightened to pat Teddy on the shoulder.

Al was surprised Teddy didn't flinch. She stood there beaming at Fergie as if she'd just handed Teddy a Nobel Prize. Teddy was able to look right at Fergie—quite a difference from the way she'd been around Cam.

When he had first met Teddy, Al had picked up a booklet on autism and had learned it was far less common in girls than in boys. For girls, the symptoms might appear as extreme shyness or anxiety, masking that they might not be responsive to the social cues of others. Autistic girls also tended to focus on topics such as on ponies, princesses, dolls, or drawings, common passions for nonautistic girls too, which made their autism harder to detect sometimes than that in boys. "Princess" had perked her right up.

Leave it to Fergie to know exactly the right thing to say to Teddy.

As soon as they were back in the truck, Fergie said, "This gives us a whole new slant on looking at Dr. Corneille."

"You don't think he's the one who made those marks on the bones, do you?"

"Of course not. But now, let's consider some facts. What do you know about organ transplants?"

"I read somewhere that on any day, over one hundred ten thousand people are waiting for an organ transplant and that eighteen people a day die because they don't get one in time."

"What is wrong with you, Al, that you'd remember that kind of detail from something you read?"

"It's more of a curse than a blessing, usually."

"Those scrapes on the bones Teddy found. Are you thinking what I'm thinking?"

"Yep."

"Who do we tell?"

"No one. We've seen what Cam's half-cocked, over-zealous efforts generated. Let's wait until we really know something."

"Where do we start?"

"Well, there's got to be paperwork and someone to fake it. Organs have to be cleared so their source doesn't have HIV or AIDS, hepatitis, jaundice, or any of that sort of thing. Nor can the organs come from someone over two hundred fifty pounds, from a body that's started to decompose, or from a drowning victim. And there'll be a money trail, although that will almost surely be masked or laundered."

"Do you think there's money enough in this to make it worth the risk?"

"You're going to squawk about my memory again, but I was working on something similar once and had to do some digging."

"I'll do what I can to keep from biffing you upside your head."

"The issue is supply and demand. It's illegal, of course, in America to buy or sell organs for transplant. Almost five thousand people died in America last year while waiting for a kidney. A black-market price for a kidney is about one hundred fifty thousand dollars. For a while, dealers were going to the Third World countries offering up to, say, five to six thousand to some poor person for a kidney, sometimes only a thousand or two, still a fortune to people in those places. Hard to ship those here, so then there were people who flew to those other countries to get their operations. In some of those countries, according to a World Health Organization report I read, as much as sixty to seventy percent of all transplant operations are to 'transplant tourists' from developed countries. And that's just for kidneys. For a liver, the stakes and prices go quite a bit higher."

"Amazing as it is you can recall all that, how does that affect what we're looking at?"

"Most hospitals don't have vigorous enough procedures for looking into the sources of the organs transplanted in their own operating rooms, and the operations are lucrative enough most aren't disposed to rock that particular boat.

They get known as 'broker-friendly' facilities. For a while, people with matching blood types from other countries were being flown just for such operations. But you can't do that with the liver, and you said your guy, Doc Corneille, has done several liver transplants this year."

"So, maybe not human trafficking but human-organ trafficking?"

"I don't know. It's possible it could be both. The mixed ethnic backgrounds of the bones—Asian, Russian, and Latino—may well suggest a tie. Add to that the age and gender of the bones, all female over thirty, and we start to get a pretty grim picture."

"Oh my. Harvesting from those not as attractive and as fresh as the incoming new stock. But are you sure?"

"Of course not. But it's the best working hypothesis I have. Think of Occam's Razor."

"That the simplest answer is best?"

"That's not quite it. Occam's Razor means of all the possible explanations, the simplest answer that covers all the circumstances is the most likely to be true. And even then, I'm keeping an open mind if we trip over any more circumstances than we have."

"I wouldn't have leaped to harvesting, but it does fit... so far."

"It could explain to me how Danielle Cassidy, the FBI's special agent heading up their push against human trafficking, got here so fast with a tactical team. They're camped out here in town and probably looking for the same thing we are now."

"You aren't going to tell her, are you?"

"Of course not. That's the whole reason Clive had the bones checked by someone local. You let the feds in on something like that, and it's like knocking over a beehive, one that doesn't give a crap about anything we might be working on. We can tell them later if we bother to tell them at all."

"Those words might have as easily come from Clayton's mouth."

"Though I don't still work for him, even on an ad hoc advisory basis, anymore, I do agree with him about that. We've worked with the feds many times in the past, and I can't remember a single instance where it was fun."

"I'm starting to see why Clayton loves you like a son."

CHAPTER FIFTEEN

A L SLOWED HIS TRUCK TO fifteen miles an hour, the limit for the loop into Austin's Bergstrom International Airport terminal. He'd been part of a group chase scene once through the old Robert Mueller Airport, which had raced through the middle of Austin, a long, exhausting pursuit with city squad cars and state-trooper cruisers mixed in. The fellow they were after, an out-of-work sheetrock hanger escaping from a domestic-abuse scene in a stolen car, had heard somewhere that airports were no-fly zones, so helicopters couldn't catch him there. With a dozen assorted police units glued to his back bumper, that point had turned out to be moot. He was soon enough sprawled on the pavement with the city cops folding him like origami.

Outside ABIA's baggage area, Al pulled over to the curb. A tall man in a dark suit, white shirt, and blue tie—all a rare sight in a climate that was already climbing for the nineties—came out and walked in brisk steps toward Al's truck. Fergie got out of the passenger side and climbed into the truck's backseat.

Doug Chandle got into the truck and tossed his lightly packed garment bag into the side of the backseat where Fergie wasn't sitting. "How're you doing, Al?" A clean-shaven man with a long, rectangular face and square chin, he held out a hand.

When he'd been a cop in uniform and later a detective, Al never once caught Doug with a five o'clock shadow, though the dark tint to his chin suggested he could grow a dandy beard if he wanted. He had the eyes of a beagle, sad most of the time, but able to show keen, raw excitement when he caught a scent.

Al shook and pulled away while Doug tugged his seat belt into place. "Just so you know, Al, I would never make a move on Fergie here, if that's what this is about."

Al glanced and saw Doug wasn't grinning. "Why would you think a thing like that?"

"Just clearing the air. So you know, no one's tried that since the days of Kerby Spence. Fellow cop. Never made it past uniform days. You recall him, don't you, Fergie?"

"Oh, yeah."

"Big fellow. Footballer. We don't know for sure what he said or did, but he later claimed Fergie grabbed him by a tender area and was dragging him around the parking lot. Some said he couldn't get free of her grip and went so far as to go for his piece, when she tased him with his own Taser. In the inevitable investigation that followed, he said he'd accidentally tased himself. Wouldn't ever look Fergie in the eye again."

"I didn't know that," Al said.

"True story," Doug said.

"Happy times," Fergie muttered from the backseat.

"Did you know the Taser was developed by a guy at NASA?" Al asked. "He named it after Tom Swift's electric rifle. You know, Thomas A. Swift's electric rifle."

"What?" Doug asked.

"It's the kind of shit I have to put up with all day long, Doug. Don't get him started," Fergie said. "Let's say we work forward, here."

"Well, then. What's so important I had to cancel my limo-service ride for this quick meet?" Doug said.

Al glanced into the rearview mirror and gave Fergie the nod to do the talking.

"First, did you get anything interesting on Dr. Corneille's stay in Houston?"

"I'd say it was all pretty uninteresting if you put aside the fact he one day just pulled up and decide to move to Austin. I guess it was the same situation as when he was in Atlanta and shifted to Houston. Maybe he just likes a change of scenery now and again. His work was good, his patients swore by him, and he made a beaucoup pile of money while he was there. When I tried to talk to the folks at the hospital, turns out they were edgy about him, wouldn't talk yet. Very odd, considering how good he was. But that could be a lot of things, probably nothing. Standard procedure. Why? What do you have?"

Al took in Doug's suit, an Armani, he was pretty sure. Al was down to one suit himself, which he saved for funerals, semiformal events, and to be buried in if it came to that. He'd taken all the others to Goodwill some years before.

"Let me pitch you a hypothesis," Fergie said. "And it's a stretch at first, so keep your mind open."

"I'm listening."

"What if Corneille was getting around the organ-donor shortage somehow in a way that would encourage patients to slip him quite a bit of extra money to be moved forward in line and get, say, a new liver?"

"What?" Doug turned around in his seat. Fergie slid to her left so he could see her. "Are you shitting me? You're darned tootin' I'd say it sounds a little fantastic. Make that a lot fantastic. I wouldn't have credited you, or Al here, with such a flight of fancy."

"It's the only way everything is explained—the bones,

the doctor, the hinky way the hospital wants us to find something out but won't say what they suspect. Don't you think a doctor might even convince himself he's doing some sort of good while making piles of money?"

Doug started to speak but stopped himself. After he'd thought a moment, he said, "Well, he would certainly make money. This could be worth millions to him as long as he's been practicing. I suppose it's feasible. And no one's caught on in all this time?"

"It would explain the moving around when a hospital finally got an inkling, and it'd also be why none of them really want to talk about what might be going on."

"How would he pull it off?"

"There'd have to be a supplier, a regular one, and a crafty one able to fudge the needed paperwork so it's good enough a hospital eager for all the transplant work wouldn't look too close."

"What's this supplier do? Just go out and murder people for their organs?"

"Let's say the person was tied to the human-trafficking biz. When the women start to get old for that sort of thing, they get harvested. Eyes, lungs, heart, kidneys, and liver all add up to a big payday if someone has a place to quickly move those. The waiting list to get organs is huge, and some people with money are willing to pay extra."

"Well, I'll be. That never came to me. Are you sure about any of this? Do you have anything like hard evidence?"

"No. But it's the most logical answer of the moment. The bones found show the markings of organ removal, but that's not enough for a conviction or even a formal investigation yet."

"You haven't let the city know, have you, or God forbid, the feds?"

"Not yet," Al said. "What we have is way too thin.

Clive Barnes, our ME, bounced what he'd found to our detectives. They didn't bite because they don't respect Teddy the way I do. Plus, my head was set right to see how all this might tie together. Just might, is all."

"Teddy?" Doug asked.

"Clive's assistant. She's a little autistic."

"Ah," Doug said, as if he understood, and maybe he did.

"It's just our harebrained idea, so far," Fergie said.

"There seems to be a lot of wiggle room between being remotely possible and being far-fetched." Doug shook his head.

"Well, you won't know until you unearth something solid," Fergie said. "Could be nothing or a very big something. But at least we have a place to put the end of the crowbar as we start prying now."

"Okay, then. I'll go to point on this." Doug turned around until he was looking forward at the road ahead. "I guess I've got my work cut out for me. I have a pile of paperwork to look into."

Al thought Doug's eyes sparkled a bit more than before. He'd caught the scent. The French detective saying used to be, "*cherchez la femme*," show me the woman. More recently, it was, "Show me the money." Doug may well have been grasping for the first time that a hefty reward fee from the hospital might be coming down the pike his way after all.

He stayed quiet the rest of the way to his house and gave just a curt wave as Fergie climbed back into the front seat and Al headed toward his own house.

High on a hill, a pair of binoculars tracked Al's truck as it pulled up in front of his house. When Al and Fergie got out of the truck and went to the door, the binoculars lowered.

Al had his hand on the front door's knob and heard Tanner bark from close inside the door. He wondered how the little fellow had gotten all the way to the door. Last he'd seen him, Tanner was curled on the bedroom rug beside the bed, still wearing his cast.

Before he could open the door, Fergie reached out and put a hand on his forearm. "I've been watching you stiffen a little as we got to the door, Al."

"Really? I didn't think that was showing."

"I mean you're tensing up when you should be glad to get home and see how Tanner is doing. Is it the business between Maury and Bonnie?"

"I'm not sure if there's anything I should or could say to them. Should I warn Bonnie? Or should I warn Maury?"

"You don't think Maury is good enough for Bonnie?"

"I didn't say that."

"Or Bonnie for Maury?"

"That either."

Fergie sighed. "Your brother has ways that differ from yours. He may take an alternate path at times, but it doesn't necessarily make his way wrong or your way right. And Bonnie's pretty capable of making decisions."

"You saying they're both adults and I should butt out?"

"I'm saying it might be best if you don't judge either of them. They might just return the favor. Maury, after all, is quite a different creature from you."

"Maury does seem to be making some progress, although it's increasingly difficult to be a rake at his age."

"Give him more credit than that. He admires you even though he's the older brother. He emulates you, to some extent. Where he flits about, you are stable and loyal. Where you are strong and forthright, he's... well, maybe not. You might consider that as he tries to change, he may or may not make it. But if you can't forgive him, then that's an issue on your plate."

Tanner barked again, just inside the door. Al wanted to swing the door open, but he paused. "When we were little, I came home from one of my first days of elementary school and told our mother about a bully who'd picked me up and wouldn't let go. I'd kicked and twisted and fought, but he was too big for me. I'd been in tears as I told Mom about how frustrated I'd been. She turned to Maury and said, 'Maurice, these boys must pick you up too, as they do Allard. What do you do?' And Maury said, 'I just hang there, and after a while, they get tired of holding me.'"

Fergie almost said something then wrestled back a smile. "Well, okay then."

Al opened the door, and Tanner, brown and white, his ears flopping in eagerness, came limping toward him like Tiny Tim at Christmas with his little crutch. Al felt a tug at his heart at how the little dog was so full of pluck and game.

"Should you be hobbling around on that cast like that?" Al reached to pick up Tanner and hold him.

"The vet said it'd be good for him to get around, that the cast will take the weight, and it'll be better for him to be active than not," Bonnie called from the kitchen, where she hovered beside the range, stirring something in a pan with a wooden spoon. Al could smell garlic, tomatoes, and some fresh basil. Maury stood at her side, making a salad.

Al admitted to himself that he hadn't really stayed at the vet's long enough to hear any instructions she'd had about Tanner's recovery.

"Oh my. That smells wonderful, Bonnie." Fergie moved closer to look down into the open pan of bubbling red.

"It's the fresh herbs and tomatoes that make the difference." Bonnie stirred the sauce and rose on her toes to glance down into the tall pot where Al guessed pasta was boiling. Maury leaned closer to Bonnie, showing her how to whip up a classic vinaigrette with a dollop of Dijon for the salad. Bonnie had come a ways since calling it "some funny frog mustard" she'd found in his refrigerator. Fergie moved away to fuss over getting the table set.

Al felt Tanner lick his hand and looked down at the dog, who grinned back up at Al. Tanner's tongue hung a quarter inch out the side of his mouth, and he seemed content and happy, for a dog just back from the vet. Al leaned closer toward him and muttered, "How did this happen? One minute I'm planning to live a happy retirement life... alone, and suddenly I have a family, full of the usual dysfunctional misfits, with a dog."

When they sat down at the table, steam and an intoxicating smell rose off the pasta dish and the mound of garlic bread next to it. *Comfort food again.* Al knew what to expect when it was Bonnie's turn to cook. If Bonnie had her way, they'd all have cute little round bellies like hers.

While he passed the salad bowl to Fergie, just to make conversation, Al said, "Hey, I forgot to tell you. A former colleague of yours finally retired early from the city police department. Fellow named Dennis Cranston. Wasn't he one of those Internal Affairs had been after for years?"

"That asshole? He was never any friend of mine. What a would-be cowboy. He was as bent as they get and a heavy-fisted thug at that. Should've been caught on something ages ago."

"I thought you wouldn't shed any tears over the guy's leaving the department. The county had to look into him for domestic abuse, twice. They never found anything solid in the corruption charges, did they?"

"No. But there was plenty of smoke to that fire."

"Well, he's out on his own hook now. Something juicy must've come along his way for him to get out of IA's hair at last."

Fergie's fork was halfway to her mouth, and she stopped, leaving a bite of pasta in midair. "When'd you hear that?"

"FBI's answer to human trafficking, Danielle Cassidy, let me know, right after grousing about what a bust the raid on the Red Barn turned out to be. There was nothing there at all."

"I don't know," Maury said. "They seemed to have missed the basement. Maybe they should have looked there."

"What basement?"

"The one in the Red Barn. It wasn't mentioned in any of the news reports of the bust I saw. Nor was my name mentioned. Thanks again for that."

"Back to the basement. What did you mean by that?"

"Yeah, I know. Almost no buildings in all Texas have basements. Usually just a slab. Never heard of one in a barn. But this place had one."

"A basement!" Al turned to stare at Fergie. "The fucking place has a basement?"

CHAPTER SIXTEEN

"WHEN THE FEDS CAME BUSTING into the place, I was still getting my initial tour." Maury glanced toward Bonnie, whose eyes opened wider, but she waited. Maury turned back to Al. "The nice little girl showing me around, Mi-Hyun, from South Korea she said, took off in a run as soon as the front door got smashed in."

"That's *all* you got time for, wasn't it?" Bonnie said.

"I told you. Nothing happened in there. There wasn't time."

"But if there had been?" Bonnie's eyes narrowed.

Al suppressed a grin and didn't look toward Fergie. Not long before, Bonnie had been keeping Maury away at a stiff arm's length.

"Anyway, I was back by this curtain, a kind of tapestry, and was thinking of hiding behind it," Maury said. "Or I could have run down this set of stairs that led down to the basement. They opened up under a ramp. Before I could decide, the ramp moved upward until it was flat, driven by some kind of hydraulic. When it was closed, the surface was covered by the same carpet as the hallway. You couldn't tell it was there. In fact, the feds came running at me right across it. They had me on the ground and were tying me into all kinds of knots right on top of it. Who would think there'd be a basement in a barn and a door able to close leading to it?"

"Why didn't you mention this earlier, to us or the FBI?"

"Well, things have been pretty topsy-turvy since I was let go by the feds. At the time, they were too brusque and busy to ask. Tanner was hurt, you'll recall, and you guys were galloping around the county. This is the first chance I've had to debrief."

"Oh, he's done some debriefing all right," Bonnie said.

"Bonnie!" The tips of Maury's ears turned pink.

"Hey, I'm not saying I'm the tramp here. That would be my sister Lucinda. Sweet old Lucy. She told Mom she got so limber by doing yoga. She didn't even know any yoga," Bonnie said, "unless you count spending most of her college years in the downward-facing-dog position."

Al cleared his throat. "Could we could return to the Red Barn having a basement, Maury?"

"Mi-Hyun hinted that, for a man of means, the downstairs was where the really good, expensive, and kinky fun could be had. Now we'll never know." He saw Bonnie glaring at him. "What?"

From the car parked high on the hill, the view of the sun going down across the lake and settling into the trees on the horizon might have been a moving sight to anyone else. However, the glare just made seeing through the binoculars harder until the sky got dark enough that one by one the lights in the house popped on. *Is it going to be a calm night at home, or are they onto something yet?*

Al has a nice house here on the lake. Give him that. As the darkness settled like a warm, damp cloak over the mountain cedar and live oak trees clustered around the car, the night noises of the woods started up. The wind rustled the top leaves of the trees.

Something rustled or slithered its way across the dry

leaves on the ground—not the herky-jerky scamper of a lizard after a bug, but something up to less good than that. *A snake, a scorpion?* Then the birds kicked into high gear with their noises.

The area around Al's house was rife with mockingbirds, the state bird of Texas. They attracted females and competed with other males by incessant calls as varied as they were loud—piercingly loud, really. The bird sounds seemed pretty at first then got louder and louder until the sky was shrieking with the calling and crowing chorus of increasingly urgent cries. The din went on and on, fueling the urge to pull out the piece and unload a clip into the trees. Then a pair of scissor-tailed flycatchers high in a nearby pecan tree started in with a noise that sounded like a group of thirty monkeys cutting up with giggles, hiccups, and chattering.

Down below, the front door opened, and Al and Fergie came out to the truck, Al carrying something, perhaps a small bag. They got into the truck. *Good. Give them a minute to get on the road, start the car, and ease out to follow at a distance. Al has too much experience for anyone to tail him closely.*

Traffic was at that halfway point between rush-hour people coming home from city jobs fighting stop-and-go traffic on the main corridors heading out of town and the more sporadic crowd of vehicles going to gyms, groceries, and bars. Al's truck slowed and turned into the parking lot of the Red Barn, his headlights lighting up the yellow police tape. The place hadn't been allowed to reopen yet. But Al was there. *Interesting. Very interesting.*

The truck sat there for a minute, then Al and Fergie got out, walked across the parking lot, ducked under one stretch of yellow tape, and went up to the front door. Al moved the tape to one side there and fiddled at the front lock. Then they both slipped inside.

Well, time for that call. Pick up the cell phone and hit the speed dial.

———◆———

Al waited a heartbeat or two in the nearly black foyer for Fergie to catch up.

"You think it's all right for us to come poking around in here?" Fergie asked. "It doesn't feel all right." She stood inside the closed door, probably letting her eyes get used to the dark.

Al didn't feel comfortable either, but he wasn't going to tell her that. The last time he'd seen that place, it had been crawling with feds in SWAT gear, just the sort of thing to give even the most law-abiding citizen the heebie-jeebies.

"We'll just be in and out."

"You always say that, but it usually takes longer."

He shook his head and grinned, though he knew she couldn't see that. He used a narrowed end of a pencil flashlight to lead the way through the building's dark interior. With industrial carpet, reinforced corners, and recessed lighting, the place was made for heavy wear and tear, just what you'd want for what had been at the very least a busy whorehouse.

Al moved forward through the lobby and into an open waiting area. The space was smaller than it had been as a dance hall. Much of the area where people used to sit and drink a cold one between dances must have been partitioned off into rooms for the building's most recent use. Fergie headed toward the tapestry-like curtain along the far right wall. Maury had said he'd been standing beside it when the FBI team came swarming in. The stairs to the basement had closed right in front of him.

"Over here," Al said in a low voice. No sense shouting even if the place was empty. "He said he saw a guy reaching here when the stairway started down."

Al shone a path of light along the floor so Fergie could come over to him. Maury was right. Once the damn thing was down and in place, he couldn't tell it wasn't just more of the same floor, and in Texas, where no one had basements, nobody would think that a barn would.

When she was beside him, they moved close to the wall. A piece of wooden trim ran along the wall about waist high with paneling below and what looked like stucco walls encrusted with occasional fake gems that glittered as his flashlight beam swept across them. *Classy joint.* He felt along the bottom of the trim, running his hand back and forth. *Nothing.* He tried again, digging in with his fingertips. Then he found a small recess, barely an inward dent with a flat toggle switch tucked away where no one would see it or even feel it unless they were searching hard. He flipped it, and the floor tilted downward like a soundless jaw opening. *Give whoever designed it credit for making it as quiet as possible.*

They moved around to where the stairs led down into the blackness but stopped to listen first. He couldn't even hear street noises. The place was well soundproofed. He pointed his beam at the flooring, and they started down. At the bottom, he saw a switch chest high on the wall and, figuring it wouldn't matter down there, flipped on the lights.

The center room was big, with a stage on one end where strippers could perform. The room could also serve as a staging area where patrons could wait on red leather sofas and chairs, each with end tables handy for holding refreshments.

He thought back to when the big dusted hardwood

floor dance area upstairs would have been a dance hall, one of Texas's many two-stepping honky-tonk kicker bars. The basement had to have been a place—not inexpensive to make—for less-attractive activities. *Who knew? A casino? A brothel?* However, the dance hall hadn't turned a profit—or perhaps it had, but someone had cut out with their money before the downstairs activities got too widely known. Maybe the basement had come later, only with the most recent owner. He looked around, trying to envision how the floor had worked. Doors lined both sides, but the one on the far end had a steel door instead of a wooden one, though it looked like the others.

"Could you hold a light?" He got out his small leather folder while Fergie kept a beam of light on the lock. He leaned close to listen as he felt and fiddled.

Click. They were in.

"If this downstairs was some countryside bordello, couldn't they have laundered the money right through the dance hall upstairs?" Fergie asked.

"I was just mulling that over. Should have worked. We might've gotten wind of it in time, though. Still, why close down then open back up? This place only got busy again recently."

The office looked more like a money-counting room than a luxury den—no swank mahogany or teak desk with bookshelves or even paintings. The walls were bare except for one oversized battery-run clock. The furniture was all stark and functional, mostly metal, straight out of some office supply store. No money had been left behind or even a scrap of paper in the waste cans. Empty electric money counters sat on a couple of the tables, and a paper shredder stood against one wall, but even it had been cleared out and emptied. When they'd been missed by the feds, whoever had been on that floor must have waited

RUSS HALL

it out until the coast was clear and then scooted with everything they could carry.

Al checked the walls—no safe or picture to hide one behind. He checked the floors, which had the same industrial gray carpet as the rest of the place—no seams or breaks.

A smaller desk sat in the back corner, its only concession to comfort a Herman Miller Aeron office chair worth as much as the rest of the furniture in the room altogether. The desk was bare except for a phone pressed against the wall at the far back right corner of it. Al lifted the receiver and saw a number but no name. According to the time stamp, the call would have come in just before or in the early moments of the raid.

"What the hell are you doing here?"

He clicked the "erase" button at the sound of the voice, which he knew wasn't Fergie's. He looked up. Danielle Cassidy stood in the doorway, wearing her dark-blue suit. Two guys, also in suits, though theirs didn't match hers, pressed into the small room. As soon as they were inside, the fourth person came in: Cam Callaghan, for the first time not in uniform. She wore a white blouse, jeans, red cowgirl boots, and her service piece in its holster strapped to her side.

The two bulky agents with her spread to either side of the door. Neither went for a badge or a gun, though they did look like they hoped Al would try to make a dash.

"Well, well, well," Danielle said. "I thought you were off the department for a while."

"Fair enough," Al said. "I thought *she* was still on it." He nodded toward Cam.

"She is, kind of. But she's helping me," Danielle said.

"I have a chance to—" Cam started.

"Let's not go into that," Danielle said. She turned back

174

to Al. "This is just the sort of thing that so turns me off about having anything at all to do with you locals." Her voice got louder, growing to a near shout. "Bunch of half-baked, half-trained..." She managed to stop herself. "I ought to take you in for interfering with an investigation."

"What investigation?" Al asked. "You tromped all around this building and missed what I found. You were done here and were going to have to turn it back over to whoever owns it. Have you found out who that is yet? I mean, after you've sorted through the usual handful of shell companies."

"That's part of our investigation. If we have anything to share with the department, we'll do so with Clayton, not you. Now tell me why I shouldn't haul you in and lock you up."

"Because if you do, I double-damn guarantee I'll call every journalist in the county who owes me a marker and tell them how good and thorough your job of looking around wasn't."

Danielle's mouth opened then closed.

Al could hear the clock on the wall. *Tick. Tick. Tick.*

A flush of color started up Danielle's cheeks. Still she said nothing.

Finally, she stirred, glanced toward Fergie then Cam, and settled on Al.

"Oh, what the hell? Just get the fuck out of here... before I change my mind."

As he and Fergie filed past them, Al figured Danielle and her men would have a long evening ahead, checking out that part of the building, which Al guessed had been swept as clean of prints or any scrap of data as it could get. They might have gotten something if they'd found the basement when they first swarmed the place, but they hadn't. *Simple as that.*

Al's eyes locked with Cam's. She glared back at him. Neither said a word. Then he and Fergie were past and heading up the stairs.

"Whew," Fergie said.

Al took his first full breath in a while and had to agree with her.

CHAPTER SEVENTEEN

AL DROVE THROUGH THE DARKNESS, heading back toward his house, feeling a little deflated but still relieved to have been let go. Traffic around them was light, with only a sporadic pair of headlights swinging past to cross his headlight beams. Fergie sat silent in the passenger seat. He didn't mind. That gave him time to think, which he liked to do in those quiet times. Maybe she knew that or sensed it, or she was as bummed as he was about their look around inside the Red Barn being curtailed the way it had been.

Back in his early years as a deputy, riding solo around in a cruiser late at night, he'd wondered from time to time just how much good he was doing. *Protect and serve.* He would pull over a speeder or clean up an accident or look around where someone's house had been broken into. *But how much of it mattered or even made a small difference?*

Some of the deputies talked about getting the bad guys. Even then, Al recognized that as a rhetorical device to help them feel like good guys in their jobs, and some of them weren't. *Ah, well.* He turned in to the drive to his house, feeling and hearing the welcome crunch of the gravel of coming home.

When he pulled up to the house, a car was sitting where he usually parked the truck.

"Now who the hell is visiting at this hour?" he asked.

"Well, taking a flying leap at the moon of a guess, I'd say it's Doug Chandle," Fergie said.

Al pulled into place behind the car and looked at her as he turned off the truck's engine.

"That's his car, anyway."

When Al swung open the front door to the house, Tanner came hobbling in a scamper toward him.

Al bent forward to sweep him up. "Should you be running around like that?"

He got a lick on the nose as an answer.

Doug sat on the couch, holding a glass of what looked to be Al's good single-malt Scotch, judging from the previously unopened bottle on the coffee table. Al rarely kept hard liquor in the house. He had been gifted the eighteen-year-old Scotch and had been saving it for a special occasion: a celebration, something like that.

Maury was holding a glass, and he looked as though he'd taken the opportunity to celebrate. Bonnie had pulled one of the dining chairs over and was holding a beer.

Bonnie stood up. "You want anything?"

Al shook his head, eased around the end of the coffee table, and sat at the other end of the couch from Doug.

"Beer," Fergie said. "But sit down. I'll get it."

With beer in hand, she dragged one of the other dining chairs over and sat beside Bonnie. "Well?" she asked.

"You first," Doug said. "Your news is bound to be better than mine."

"I doubt it," Fergie said. She told them about their going to the Red Barn and getting into the basement, only to be caught by Danielle, two other agents, and Cam.

"Why, that little traitor," Bonnie said. "Was she following you or something?"

"Of course she was," Al said.

"You guys are lucky the feds didn't lock you up and

throw the key away." Doug took a sip from his glass. His eyes looking over the rim of the glass seemed a little closer together than Al remembered, and they were narrowed.

Al had known Doug for years, all the way back to when Doug had quit being a city detective to hang up his shingle as a PI. Some cops quit because they burned out, but not Doug. He was ambitious but wasn't progressing quickly enough, to his thinking. Most of Doug's work had been in the city, so Al hadn't had to deal with him much. But when Al had, he felt the usual professional-law-enforcement's love of people in the private sector butting in, which amounted to grimacing tolerance at best. Doug had been occasionally pushy, and that didn't help. Still, once or twice he had done some good and helped a stalled case, so Al sought to keep his mouth closed and his mind open.

"Why'd you come over at this hour?" Fergie took a sip from her beer. "Your news about the job couldn't wait until morning?"

"That's the news," he said. "That there's no job anymore. I left a check on the dining table for you."

"Men usually leave the money on the dresser," Bonnie said.

"You're thinking about the kind of business that was in that Red Barn place," Maury said.

"I told you not to talk about going there." Bonnie started to stand.

Fergie put a hand on her shoulder and eased Bonnie back onto her chair. "Not now, guys." She turned back to Doug. "What'd you find?"

"It's what I didn't find," he said.

Tanner tensed up and quivered in Al's hands. Al looked down. Tanner was staring at Doug, not barking or sharing any expression, just staring, as if getting a good picture of him in his mind—the minds and memories of dogs, after all, originated before the days of Polaroid film. That was the first Tanner had acted that way, like a Geiger counter crackling over uranium.

"And what was that?" Fergie asked.

"Any wrongdoing by Dr. Corneille. I had my hopes up. The woman at the hospital who hired me did too. Her instincts were what started the task. But it turns out to be nothing. Tempest in a teapot."

"Really? The paperwork was pristine?" Al rubbed behind Tanner's ear and felt a lump there from his night on the home-defense team.

Tanner didn't look up but stayed fixed on Doug and quivered.

"I checked it thoroughly. I even paid the good doctor a visit. He charmed my socks off by being as open and transparent as anyone could want."

"You saw the paperwork," Al said. "Where do the organs come from? The ones Corneille uses?"

Doug sighed, sneaked a peek at his wristwatch, and took another sip of the eighteen-year-old Scotch.

"There are half a dozen places in Austin where one can obtain organs, but it's not like the organs are usually just sitting around on shelves. There's a cryobank, a nonprofit organ-saving alliance, and the other usual places. Corneille gets his from LEBC Biologicals. They have an office here now, and it's the same outfit he's used for years, he tells me. And, yes, it's a legitimate place. Small suite of cinder-block stuccoed buildings out past the airport."

"I wonder why they'd locate out there," Al said, "with most of the hospitals in a pretty tight group along with other medical complex buildings downtown."

"I don't know." An edge crept into Doug's voice. "Maybe the land is cheaper. It'd have to be, with 737s coming in and out over your head all day. Could be they have to be close to where organs get shipped in and out."

"I'm sorry. I was just thinking out loud." Al glanced at his watch. "Well, if that's that on the case, so it goes. It was good to see you again, Doug."

Some of the stiffness eased out of Doug like sand pouring from his socks. He knocked back the rest of Al's Scotch, put the glass on the coffee table, and rose. He held out a hand.

Al shook hands, as did Fergie, and she led him toward the door.

Maury gave a half wave, yawned, and went to go downstairs. Bonnie was rinsing out glasses in the sink when Fergie came back.

"How was he to work with?" Al asked.

"Hard to tell. I haven't been with him long enough to get a feel for him as a partner."

"What's your gut tell you?"

"I'd rather not say."

"That says a lot on its own. Don't think he could cut it on our little team, do you?"

"Can you picture him sitting out all night on a stakeout, eating beef jerky?" Fergie asked.

"I can't picture him as the beef-jerky type," Bonnie said. "The jerky type, but not the beef-jerky type." She tossed the towel onto the counter and headed for the stairway downstairs.

"I think that's what Tanner thought, too," Al said. "If this dog shaking like a maraca was any indication, ol' Dougie flunked the Tanner lie-detector test."

Fergie tilted her head at Al, who still sat on the couch, rubbing Tanner's head. "Really? You think Doug might lie about something like that and pay me good money for the privilege of doing so?"

Al nodded. "I don't know Doug all that well. But doesn't it seem a pretty short period of time for Doug to have tracked all this down and checked it out when, prior to this, he's been like a snail carrying two overloaded suitcases?"

"You're not done with this yet, are you?" she asked.

"Hell, no," he said. "Man drinks my Scotch and then shines us along like that."

"He didn't discourage you in the least?"

"Tell you the truth, I was starting to have serious doubts about this harebrained hypothesis of mine. It was a stretch. But Doug's little trip out here has done more to encourage me than anything we've found so far."

"If he's lying, what's that make his role in this?"

"That, my lanky redhead, is part of what we're going to have to find out."

"And if he's shooting straight?"

"Then we're farther off and in worse shape than I think."

"But why would he go to the bother and risk of misguiding us and trying to get us to drop the case?"

"I don't know. I just don't know."

She shook her head. "And what will Clayton do if he finds you still messing around with this?"

"Don't know that either."

"There seems to be a whole lot you don't know."

"It has been ever thus." He shared a grin. "But finding out is going to be some kind of fun. And I usually do... find out."

Al woke to hear Fergie in the shower and guessed that ruled out a morning quickie. *Did they really need one after what had turned into a minor marathon in the sheets the previous night?*

Tanner whined low and stood beside the door.

"Okay. I get you, subtle though you are." Al pulled on his pants and went to let Tanner outside. The little fellow sure got around well for a dog with one leg in a cast. Al remembered the one time he'd had a cast, way back when they were heavy, white, and made of plaster, not like the blue padded-inside fiberglass thing Tanner wore. Al could still feel the itch that had pestered and gnawed inside the cast until he'd had to straighten out a coat hanger to reach down inside to where it itched.

"Where are you and the string bean galloping off to today?" Bonnie asked when Al trickled into the dining area. She was stacking pancakes onto a plate. She was from the old school and had a bottle of real maple syrup warming up in a pan of water. The smells filled the area while Al sipped his coffee, eager to be on his way but aware that he had a household now and even the early mornings were occasions for discussion, the feast of reason.

"Well, other than maybe having to revisit everything we know, we're off to pay a visit to a techy pal of mine, Meat Jenkins. He's got the day off as the department alpha geek. He's what we need just now."

"Is that polite, Al, calling a guy 'Meat'?" Maury had just come up the stairs from the guest quarters.

Fergie came out of Al's bedroom, ready for the day. She wore tight blue jeans tucked into brown boots that came nearly to her knees, with a white blouse over which her long, flowing red hair fluttered and glistened.

"Whooee," Bonnie said. "Sometimes, you make me wish I was a lipstick lesbian, for sure."

"Hey, I'm sitting right here," Maury said. Before Bonnie could give him a snappy comeback, he turned to Al. "I guess it'd be even worse if this Meat Jenkins you were going to see was a woman."

Bonnie biffed him up the back side of his head with

a soft pot holder. "What do you have to go on that the charming Doug didn't uncover in his sleuthing?" she asked Al. "I saw the check he left for Fergie. Seems like he paid way too much for her doing very little."

"I worked. Just not as hard as the check indicated." Fergie tossed her red hair back over her shoulders.

"We've got a suspicion," Al said.

"That's all you've got?" Bonnie shook her head. "Just a suspicion?"

"There's something else. Al has a phone number," Fergie said. "From a phone he found in the Red Barn's basement."

"A place I discovered, I humbly submit," Maury said.

Fergie cocked her head at Al. "Why'd you erase the phone number in the first place and keep it back from them? From the FBI?"

"It was a snap judgment of the moment. If whoever it was coming down the stairs and finding us was whoever owned the building, I wouldn't want them to know we'd seen anything. If it was who it turned out to be, the FBI led there by Cam trailing me, that just plain pissed me off. They'd have had to put the tongs to me before I'd have shared anything after that."

———◆———

Twenty minutes later, out the door and with more sugar in her belly than she needed, Fergie watched the Texas countryside flow by as Al drove them toward Meat Jenkins's home.

The warmth of the sun seeped in through the windshield. That and the bigger-than-normal breakfast filling her stomach made her half drowsy and contemplative. Hard to believe, watching Al steer through the traffic, that he had turned out to be so confident and sure. She could still recall that moment when she had stood before him in a prom gown, one that she and her mom had taken far too long to pick out. The straps were thin as strings, and he held a corsage, a cymbidium surrounded by two red rosebuds and baby's breath. His mom must have picked that out. He'd looked at her, at the expanse of bare shoulder and upper hinting slope of breast, and he'd turned redder than those roses. Finally, he just handed her the damn thing. It was all her mother could to keep from doubling over and laughing out loud. Fergie had laughed herself when telling her gal friends. The date hadn't gone well. *But look at his confidence now.* He must've brought some of that back from whatever he'd done in the military and didn't talk about. Hard to believe he was the same man as that once-blushing boy.

She thought she knew where they were headed until Al swung the truck into the edge of Austin long enough to find one of the HEB groceries. She didn't ask but just went inside with him and followed as he headed right to the store's bakery. He pointed out a turtle cheesecake, thick with caramel, chocolate, and pecans.

She said, "You have got to be kidding me."

"It's not for us," he said. "Not after that breakfast."

As they got back into Al's truck, Fergie said, "Okay, this guy Meat is going to turn out to be skinny as a pipe cleaner, right? That's usually the way. Call a guy Slim if he's huge or Chunky if he's a rail."

"You mean like Pudge Simmons, the deputy who may not weigh a hundred?"

"Yeah, like that."

"I'll let you find out how that theory holds up."

Forty minutes later, they pulled up a lane to a house that sat alone in the sun in the middle of a two-acre lot—no trees, no garden, no fence around the yellow-sided box of a house with a single-car garage. It was probably a two-bedroom, one-bath home, though she was no real-estate agent. The land was cheaper in the area, and that Meat fellow didn't so far seem a lover of nature or aesthetics. *But, what the hell.* She fought to hold back any judgment.

Meat swung the door open to Al's knock, and Fergie did all she could not to gasp. There stood a man who had fought a battle with hair growing everywhere and lost—had also fought a battle with food and lost. He was young—well, younger than she and Al. His black hair was a tangle of unregulated curls that shot out in several directions. The black hair extended to his face, long sideburns, and mustache, with what looked like flecks of egg on the ends, and a chin and cheeks he'd shaved within a week that had grown back nearly solid black again. Five foot six and a good three-fifty. He wore sweatpants, sneakers, and a yellow T-shirt enough sizes too small that a hairy belly button stuck out, exposed beneath the bottom of the shirt. Worse, the tired, sweaty smell of the house or the man swept out toward her even though they still stood in the open air outside the house. He was clearly a man who lived alone out of some self-fulfilling prophecy. He grinned, and Fergie was startled by white sparkling teeth, quite a contrast to the last time she'd seen Toby Buchanan.

"Meat, this is Fergie. Fergie, Meat. Meet Meat." Al hadn't been able to resist that last little bit, but it didn't seem to bother Meat, who held out a hand the size of a small ham.

"Why don't you bring the laptop out onto the deck?" Al said. He handed Meat the box holding the cheesecake.

"Really? There's a bit of wind gonna kick up." He was looking down at the cheesecake.

"That's okay. We like wind," Al said. "Makes Fergie here feel like she's in ZZ Top."

Meat managed to look up long enough to share a bashful grin. "Okay."

Al grabbed Fergie's hand. She took a deep breath of air and held it as Al yanked her along through the inside of Meat's house. As they whizzed through the living room, she got a whirlwind look at the droppings of dirty clothes, empty potato-chip bags, squashed soda cans, and a medley of other sad remnants of snacks all over the place, forming a Jackson Pollock sort of painting that Fergie was going to have a hard time shaking out of her memory.

Al slid the glass door and then the screen door open and tugged Fergie outside until they stood on a wooden deck. She gulped breaths of the clean outdoors air, quite refreshing after the warm, moist air that had enveloped them while dashing through Meat's man cave.

A much-used grill took up one corner of the deck. A black plastic bag lay on the deck's wooden boards beside it, with used paper plates peeking out. An octagonal wooden table with built-in picnic benches sat in the middle of the deck. A red-and-white-striped umbrella cast a shady patch across the table. Al eased Fergie down on the shadiest side and glanced around—not much to see that she hadn't already noted. The land behind the house had occasional patches of bunch grass surrounded by expanses of brown dirt. Apparently, Meat wasn't into the suburban lawn-care scene.

Meat came out the back door, carrying a notebook computer he already held open and going. He sat down on one side of the table, which creaked but was held in place by bolts wisely installed to anchor it to the deck, not just to keep the wind from blowing it away.

Fergie was close enough to see the computer's screen but also enough downwind from Meat that she would have to endure only occasional whiffs of his unique aroma.

She'd been trying to figure out what it reminded her of. Stale, rotting cheese was the closest she'd come up with thus far.

"If I give you a phone number, is there a way you can find its owner?" Al said.

"Hell, yes. Unless it's a TracFone, some prepaid disposable, or one patched through about a zillion satellites. Don't laugh. That's happened more than once."

Fergie noticed a bit of turtle cheesecake stuck to the corner of Meat's thick lips, so obviously some of Al's bribe had already bitten the dust—or at least been bitten by Meat.

"Just for chuckles, not that I plan on giving back your delicious bribe, but why didn't Detective Ferguson here run the number through any of her old friends at the city police department?" Meat tilted his head an inch.

"Let's just say we're both trying to stay under the radar with this until we know what we've got." Al glanced to Fergie, who looked away, in part to catch a breath of fresh air. "You're my friend from the county department, but I'm asking you to keep this under your hat. I'll let Clayton know if it turns into anything."

"Ah, espionage. I like the notion of that." Meat grinned.

Fergie didn't know where Al kept coming up with such quirky folks whom he could draw upon. When she'd been a detective for the city police, she'd had her share of snitches, regular offenders, and earthy street types, but Al's contacts ran to a wider array of talents and peculiarities. This one, for instance. At least he and Meat had ties through the sheriff's department.

Al told Meat the number, and Meat's sausage-like fingers danced like excited mice across the keys. The man could type like Liberace on the piano, despite his size.

"Well, I'll be," Meat said.

"Some hidden identity?" Al asked.

"No. Just kind of a weird name. Uriah Voltag. You remember a rock band called Uriah Heep, Al? Before my time. But you might recall them."

"Yeah. I remember them. Fergie's old enough to know of them as well."

"Oh, say it isn't so." Meat turned to Fergie.

"Are you flirting with me, Meat?"

"I would be if I thought it would get me anywhere." He grinned. Some of the turtle cheesecake was stuck to those shiny teeth.

It took everything Fergie had not to shudder.

"Now, the big question," Al said. "Can you get a GPS fix on this phone?"

"Sure. You probably know cell phones put out a constant RF output so they can be tracked using the tower-triangulation method."

He looked ready to go into greater detail, but Al held up a hand, so Meat just added, "I can even set it up so you can track it with your cell phone."

"That's what I'm after." Al took his cell phone out and put it on the table.

Meat drew it closer and tapped away. Fergie glanced toward Al. He didn't wink or anything, just staying fixed on Meat, who for a minute and a half, held the tip of his tongue in his teeth so it stuck out on one side.

"There you go." Meat slid Al's phone back to him.

Al held it up so Fergie could see the blinking dot on a cross-grid of streets.

"Now, the big question," Al said. "Is there any of that cheesecake left?"

"Well, yeah. A little. You and the lady didn't want any, did you?" His tone was that of a child about to have a toy taken away.

"Nope. It's all yours, Meat. We've got to go. Things to do."

Meat grinned at them widely, with even more bits of cheesecake, nuts, and caramel showing all across his very white teeth. Fergie wished he hadn't provided that memory for her to carry away.

CHAPTER EIGHTEEN

A L HAD NO WAY OF knowing what to expect, so he'd brought them all along. He winked at Fergie, who also seemed glad for the extra company.

"Didn't Clayton warn you off this case?" Maury asked.

"Yeah. That's what makes it fun." Al glanced at Maury in the rearview mirror. He couldn't see Tanner but knew Maury held Tanner on his lap, already fastened to his leash.

"How're we doing?" Al asked Fergie, who was holding his cell phone.

"Still following the bouncing dot," she said. "You're headed right toward it."

"We shoulda brought more ammo," Bonnie said. "And why'd we wait until night? It's as dark as the inside of a cow out there."

"You've got two clips, Bonnie, and I'm hoping you don't fire a single shot," Al said. "You're along because you're the marksman of us, but I want you to hesitate real hard before you squeeze off at anything. Hear?"

He took her silence as a nod.

"We had to wait until he moved," Al said. "The phone was in one place all day. Now, he's on the go. That's what we want."

"I can't believe a thing like human trafficking even exists," Bonnie said.

"Well, it does," Fergie said. "And I guess we can't fault Agent Danielle Cassidy for getting a little obsessive, though she's swung all the way over to Ahab and the whale, as Al likes to put it. He's never keen on anyone being as obsessive as he can get. But all the same, thousands of young women, and even young boys, are being pulled out of some pretty sad circumstances to find out they're in worse ones here. The thing is, the victims aren't the ones to complain most of the time. It's still a better life than they had."

Bonnie huffed, too outraged to speak.

Tanner let out a matching little "Whuff."

"Yet it's slavery." Al's eyes didn't leave the road. "Pure and simple. People bought and sold. Worse, when they get too old to be pretty, apparently, they're chopped up for spare parts." His jaw tightened.

"Are you sure?" Maury said. "That sounds horrible."

"We don't have the hard evidence we need, but it's the only way this makes sense so far," Fergie said.

"It *is* horrible if it's true," Bonnie said. "Someone's gotta do something."

"Up ahead, take a right," Fergie said.

As soon as Al did, the headlights swept across a big sign on the chained and padlocked gates of a nine-foot-high chain-link fence.

"A landfill," Bonnie said. "There're gonna be rats. I told you I shoulda brought more ammo."

"No shooting at rats," Al cautioned. "We're to be as quiet as we can be."

Even Tanner got the message and didn't bark, though he strained at the leash Maury held.

Al led the way, the beam from his pen flashlight a yellow-white needle running along the base of the chain-link fence. His Sig Sauer pressed against the middle of his back inside his belt, and he hoped he wouldn't need it. Bonnie had his Glock, and Fergie carried a Smith & Wesson .38. Maury held Tanner's leash but no gun— hadn't wanted one.

Al stopped. Fergie bumped into him, and from the feel of it, Bonnie bumped into her, and Maury into Bonnie. Al held the flat of a hand back to them. Fergie peered over his shoulder. He pointed his beam of light at a stretch of chain link along a corner post, where someone had used a bolt cutter to open a four-foot-high tent flap of it. Al swung his beam to the right until he found a silver Dodge minivan parked near a low building at the edge of a parking lot twenty yards away.

"You had better stay at the vehicle," Al told Bonnie.

"But then I won't get to—" she whispered.

"Shoot anybody?" Al whispered. "I hope not. But in case we need it, you're the best shot. Think of yourself as the rear guard."

"Well, I got the rear for it." She chuckled low and started across toward the vehicle.

He lifted the flap of cut fence so Fergie and Maury could bend and slip inside one by one. Tanner scampered through, cast and all, already getting a kick in his stride, his nose twitching away.

"Whew," Maury said when Al joined them. "Landfills are sure ripe."

"This is a step up from Al's last social engagement," Fergie whispered.

"Quiet, guys," Al said. "From here forward."

Al started to take the lead, but Tanner was pulling at his leash until his collar nearly choked him. Maury had to step lively to keep up. He went out and around Al and Fergie. They had to break into a near trot to keep up.

Tanner followed a path between uneven mounds and

across material recently tamped into place by a dozer. The smells mingled, never getting much better, even though the breeze picked up and brushed against Al's face as he trotted. He fell in behind Fergie, who had always been a better runner.

Tanner barked.

"Up here!" Maury yelled.

Al huffed up until he came up to where Fergie had stopped beside Maury. Both their beams pointed to a rise. At the top of the mound, a man with the pale skin of a cadaver stood frozen in their lights, holding a shovel above a large black plastic bag that lay on the ground. He was skinny enough to look like a skeleton with clothes, and he rocked back from their lights as if they were lasers. He dropped his shovel, turned, and ran.

"Don't turn Tanner loose!" Al yelled.

Even in a cast, the dog was brave enough to be first on the scene, and Al didn't want him kicked again.

Fergie passed Maury and was moving away from Al, gaining distance with those long legs of hers. *Fine long legs.*

He caught a glimpse of the man, who was running, angling back toward the hole in the fence. Fergie took an angle on that and stretched her stride to head him off, but he was running with the fuel of raw panic. He was halfway through the hole when Fergie got there and grabbed at him. His thin nylon jacket came off in her hands, and he shot away in a full run, heading out of their lights.

Fergie wrestled her way through the hole, then Al. Maury and Tanner brought up the rear. Tanner barked steadily, the first time Al had ever heard him do so.

"You're a regular little hunting dog, aren't you?" he called back then ran to catch up with Fergie, though that was futile, given she was at full speed.

She was standing still, light pointed down at the ground when Al came panting up beside her. He bent forward and put a hand down on one knee, huffing in hard gulps of breath. He aimed his light where hers pointed.

Bonnie had the little guy's arm up behind his back and was sitting on him.

Maury and Tanner came up beside them, and Maury dropped down to pat Tanner and calm him, though he kept barking.

"You said not to shoot him," Bonnie said. "It would've been easier to do. He gave me a little tussle for half a sec."

Al reached into his pocket, took out his cell phone, and punched in a number he knew all too well.

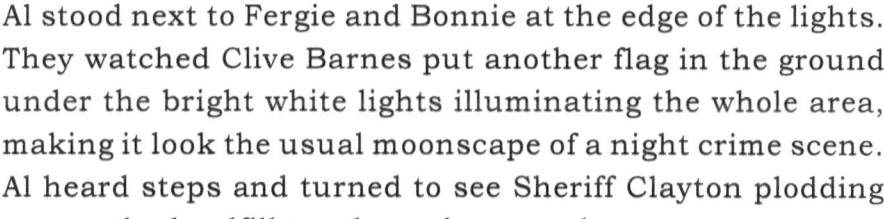

Al stood next to Fergie and Bonnie at the edge of the lights. They watched Clive Barnes put another flag in the ground under the bright white lights illuminating the whole area, making it look the usual moonscape of a night crime scene. Al heard steps and turned to see Sheriff Clayton plodding across the landfill to where they stood.

At the far extreme of the grounds, combing the landfill, Clarence caught sight of Al and waved a hand his way. He went back to work with a small rake near one of the flags, picking at the scab that was the surface of the refuse.

"I don't suppose you take this as violating my instructions to leave all this the hell alone, do you?" Clayton asked.

Al turned to look at him. "Clive's found three bodies so far. Don't know if there are any more. Teddy's borrowed Tanner, and they're looking for more." Al suppressed a shiver, though he didn't feel all that cold.

Clayton looked over toward members of the crime-scene crew digging at the flagged spots and Teddy scampering across the landfill mounds, holding Tanner's leash, with Maury jogging along behind.

"Now, don't she look just as happy looking for corpses in a landfill at night as some little girl who just got a brand-new pink dress," Clayton said.

"She has happier days than most of us."

"Probably."

"She does seem to enjoy the hunt," Al said. "And corpses don't bother her the way they might others."

"She's a wonder, all right. Now, let's talk about you."

"What about me?"

"Maybe it's high time you skedaddled out of here."

"Why?"

"That Agent Cassidy has been roused up, and she's headed this way, and I suspect her stinger's not set for stun. They'll have the full crew, corpse-smelling dogs and the lot, here any minute. You'll be doing yourself a favor by making yourself scarce by the time she arrives."

"Did Cam let her know?"

"Cam's on administrative leave. I suspect she's aiming for an invitation to Quantico, to try out to be an agent," Clayton said. "And you're retired. Now git."

Clayton looked in the holding cell and saw the little fellow huddled against the table, head bowed, as miserable looking as a wet cat just fished out of a creek. Uriah Voltag had pale, almost gray skin, deeply etched into a resigned frown and with hardly any hair on top, just a few discouraged strands in the middle going whichever way they wanted. He was starvation skinny. His hands looked as brittle as those of the corpse he had been found with, as well as the others pulled out of the landfill.

Neither Clayton nor any of the others had been able

to get a single word out of him, though they suspected he understood English. Clayton was torn. Back in the day in New York City, at what was known as "The Tombs," the Manhattan Detention Complex, the jail in lower Manhattan on 125 White Street, the story was that cops down in the basement would beat information out of suspects with a rubber hose or worse. Clayton really wanted whatever was in the recesses of that underfed head—but no rubber hoses. Kindness wouldn't work either. He had no leverage with someone like that.

Clayton felt certain the man was responsible for all the bones and bodies they had found. He might not have been the cause of their deaths, but he'd been the final messenger, the carrier, the death angel that took them to their resting places. He served someone so devotedly that he would or could say nothing. Doing what he'd done appeared to be his whole life. Clayton suspected he had nothing outside of that. He was quivering and staring down, not necessarily in remorse, but just waiting for the same bitter end he'd seen handed out to so many others. He was a whipped dog waiting for the final crack of the whip.

The sheriff had seen the type before, all too often: the loyal little guy who does all manner of disgusting grunt work but in the end is expendable to the person he nearly worships. He would never talk even though his world just took a horrible downward turn, as it inevitably had to. Clayton had seen genuine sympathy show through on Al's face when he brought him in, no matter what Uriah had done. The sad little guy was as much a victim as the corpses he lugged off to dispose of. Al had known people like that always existed, who devoted their lives to someone or something but who mattered not a whit to the ones they served. The prisons held their share of that sort, and most stayed as loyal, true, and every bit as abandoned there.

When two of his deputies came to take Uriah away, Clayton told them, "Take it easy on him. Okay?"

"You sure?"

"You heard me," he said.

"What do you do when you have a good dog that has the scent?" Fergie looked around their dining table at each of her housemates. Al's hair was still wet after coaxing Tanner into the shower to get the landfill stink off him.

"You let him run," Maury said. The sun was up outside, but none of them had been to bed yet.

"You think that's what this is about?" Bonnie said. "That Clayton has a case of the green-apple nasties because the feds are stomping all over his turf without so much as a howdy-do?"

"He can't like it," Fergie said.

"And Al's the dog, right?" Bonnie got up to go get the coffee thermos.

"Yep," Fergie said as Tanner looked up at her from where he rested on the floor with his paws across Al's boot. "Well, one of them."

"I witnessed firsthand how eager these FBI guys seem. But how's that rattle the sheriff's chain?" Maury said.

Fergie finished off the rest of the coffee in her mug. "This Cassidy, who is heading up the FBI's push against human trafficking, works for Bryan C. Richards, the special agent in charge of the Houston FBI Field Office, the biggest FBI office in Texas. He's pretty careful and conservative. She's the one who's ambitious. They've taken big bites out of human trafficking in Houston, and that's no easy job. As a port city, Houston has the highest rate of human trafficking of cities in Texas. But if they've cleaned up a lot of those places, now maybe Cassidy is looking for new conquests. I think she's hungry, too hungry, and knows how to play an equally hungry person, Cam, like someone's borrowed banjo."

"Clayton may have been giving Cam enough rope to hang herself." Al, though tired, managed a grin.

"How do you know it isn't the other way around, that she's the one being allowed to run and you're getting the rope?" Maury asked.

"You'd better put the coffee for Fergie and me in 'to-go' cups, Bonnie," Al said. "We're off to the hospital to have a chat or two."

"Don't you trust the story that Doug fellow gave you?" Maury reached over to grasp Tanner's collar so he wouldn't try to follow Al.

"He came up with his answers real fast and real pat," Al said. "Might as well give a second glance to the ones he got the answers from."

Al got up, and Fergie followed him to the bedroom, ignoring the low wolf whistle Maury let out.

Al got into his suit, the one he expected be buried in one day, while Fergie pulled on her most businesslike skirt and blouse. She wore black flats—just as well, so she wouldn't tower over Al too much. For a second or so while they were changing and she was bending and tugging, taking things off that long, lithe form of hers, his resolve nearly wavered. But a quick, stern look from her kept him on track. They came back out to the dining area looking either very businesslike or as though they were headed to church.

Bonnie held out two thermos cups of coffee. Al's thermos had a leaping trout on the side. Fergie's was shaped like a Starbucks Venti cup, only made of sturdier stuff.

"You should hunt up a nurse named April Manners," Bonnie said. "Don't let her name fool you. She's no spring chicken. She's more of an autumn turkey. But she used to be in on about every operation that Dr. Corneille ever did."

Al looked back as they headed for the door. Tanner was tugging at the grip Maury had on his collar. "Keep the place safe, buddy," Al said. "You're in charge now."

Whether the dog understood or not, he sat down and looked up at Bonnie and Maury.

***

The first thing Al thought on seeing her was that Bonnie had been right about April Manners. She looked as if she'd been built before the hospital and about as soundly. A wide, solid woman, her eyes looked alert and keen, a piercing blue. Her hair was as white as hair can get. The skin of her face and neck had more wrinkles than a topographical map of the Rockies. But her look said she didn't brook a fool gently, and the jury was still out on Al and Fergie. She was one of those people who managed always to look perpetually busy. She stood behind the nurses' station clutching three metal case files. She glanced at her watch. "I can give you three and a half minutes. Visitors' waiting room, end of the floor, pronto."

The visitors' room held a dozen chairs and one red Naugahyde sofa. The magazines scattered on the end tables were rumpled and used by who-knew-how-many hands. Al and Fergie were barely in the room when the click of approaching heels announced April Manners's arrival.

"You've assisted Dr. Corneille in most of his operations, right?" Al asked the moment Nurse Manners came into the room.

"Right." Crisp. Her mouth puckered, and her eyes narrowed.

"He does a lot of operations and manages, I hear, to get his hands on the best organs possible. He must rank to pull that off."

The resistance in her face melted. "I will say that the organs he uses are the freshest I've ever seen. And I've stood beside a kidney transplant where the organ is removed from one living human and put into another. These organs are almost that fresh. Dr. Corneille has real good connections and transport is all I can say. We're lucky to have him."

"Must be LEBC Biologicals," Al said.

"Nope. That's where we used to get them. Dr. Corneille uses Koenig Lab." Her grin had a bit of a smirk to it. She seemed happy to straighten Al out.

CHAPTER NINETEEN

A L HAD TO STEP LIVELY to keep up with Fergie and those long legs of hers.

"You poured on the syrup there after you got what you wanted." Fergie pushed out through the hospital doors and headed for Al's truck. "One minute, she looked like she wanted to bite you, the next she was purring and grinning. My stars. I'm going to have to watch that silver tongue of yours."

He started to say something but stifled it, chuckling instead.

She gave his shoulder a shove. "Men. I know where your mind went. Twist anything you say. Bunch of perverts."

They climbed into his truck, and the cab was like the early stages of a pizza oven. He turned the AC on high.

"Aren't you about bone tired?" She looked closely, noting that his eyes showed it most.

"Yeah, but we're heading toward the home stretch. I hope."

"What's next on our dance card?"

"We call on the good doctor himself. His office is in the medical complex practically across the street."

The truck had barely had a chance to shake off the heat and the dashboard to cool enough to be touched when they pulled into a space in the lot in front of a building that looked to be made of the same brick as the hospital.

They got out of the truck. The growing heat of the day slapped at Al, even though he stood in the partial shade of a tall mountain laurel bush, with seedpods hanging from it like giant string beans. A black grackle high in its branches scolded them with its *craaagk, craaagk* and an indignant flutter of its wings.

"I hope you're better at this than I am," Al said. "Acting was never something that held much appeal to me. You may have to carry us here."

"We'll see," Fergie said. "I've faked enough orgasms. I suppose I can handle this."

Al led the way across a brick path to the crosswalk and under an overhang leading to the foyer. Inside, they checked a glass-encased list of doctors' offices and got into the elevator. Al touched the fourth-floor button.

Dr. Corneille's suite of offices turned out to be practically across the hall from the elevator. The door stood open. A makeshift sign generated on a printer had been taped to the door. It read No Business Hours Today. But the open door more than hinted that someone was there. Fergie glanced at Al, who nodded. They entered a reception area with chairs and the usual magazine racks along the walls and a closed reception nurse's window.

Al could hear a low murmur of voices coming from behind the closed swinging door leading to the back. He tapped on the wood, and the voices stopped. Nothing. He pushed inside, holding the door open as Fergie followed. The door swung shut behind them.

A man stepped out of a doorway midway down the short hallway and stared at Al and Fergie. He wore a light-blue short-sleeved shirt, khaki slacks, and burgundy loafers that had probably temporarily replaced his golf cleats. The rest of his golfing outfit was right out of the window

of the Jos. A. Banks store, at least the last time Al glanced
that way into the shop's display as he had walked by.

"We're closed. Please call the receptionist and come
back another time," the man said. His hair was going to
salt and pepper, but he was in pretty good shape for his
years. His posture looked erect and confident and his
gaze unflinching, and his clean-shaven face showed the
impatient beginning of a scowl, like the captain of a ship
on which people stepped lively when he said to do so.

"This is quite urgent. You're Doctor Corneille, aren't
you?" Fergie asked, though Al was aware she already
knew that.

Dr. Corneille nodded.

Fergie pressed on. "We've had some very bad news about
Al's liver, and we hear there's a list. Look, he drinks. We'll
be the first to admit it. But he'll be dead before things ever
get around to—"

"I really can't talk with you right now." Dr. Corneille's
mouth tightened at the corners, and his eyebrows drew
closer together.

"That's all right, Dr. Corneille." A man pushed past
where the surgeon blocked the doorway. "I must go." The
man was shorter than Corneille and had dark hair and a
dark beard and mustache. His swarthiness was offset by
the three-piece pinstripe gray suit he wore with a white
shirt and a burgundy tie that matched his wingtips. Al
didn't see many suits in Texas during summer months,
particularly ones with a vest. He considered how toasty it
was getting outside. The man must have had one hell of
an air conditioner in his car.

He pressed by Al and Fergie then walked at a brisk
clip. If Corneille was a ship's captain, Al wouldn't put
the man down as his first mate but rather the captain of

another equally austere vessel. Al glanced toward Fergie. She sensed the little crackle of electricity in the air too.

"Oh, come in then. But let's make this brief. I'm having a day of constant interruptions." Corneille pivoted and went back into his office, with Al and Fergie hurrying after him before he changed his mind.

Though some doctors were known for their long-suffering patience, Corneille didn't appear to be one of those. His eyes slid to a wall clock as he indicated a couple of chairs in front of the desk he stood behind. He lowered himself into his chair while Fergie and Al settled. A diploma from the Cal Saint Marymount med school hung among the framed certificates on the wall behind the desk. He was probably looking at the same diploma Doug Chandle had seen. As Fergie had described it, the office, like the man's landscaping, seemed to have been done by someone else, who had an eye for being impersonal.

"You've just learned you're going to need a replacement liver?" he asked Al.

Fergie answered for Al. "He's known for some time this was coming, drinking the way he does, but he's been an ostrich with his head in the sand. Now, time is of the essence. We have the money, just not the time."

Al had met a few people with old money, and he always liked the story where someone asked them where they got their money. One huffy woman had answered, "We don't *get* our money. We *have* our money." He sought to carry that expression of confident entitlement, but he was acting and knew it was a stretch.

Corneille's eyes clicked slowly across their faces, mapping every nuance. He was clearly a brilliant man who missed little. Al would have been willing to bet the doctor could have told them what each of them was worth, to the nearest penny. He could probably also tell Al exactly how much Al drank, which wasn't very much at all, come to that.

"What exactly did you have in mind?"

"We thought there might be some way around the waiting list. I mean, well, you know, if we paid." Fergie managed a little emotional catch to her voice.

Corneille put his elbows on his desk and formed a steeple with the fingers of both hands. He brought the steeple to his lips and spoke through it. "Had you heard that was possible?"

"Well, no," Fergie said. "We just hoped."

Corneille lowered his hands flat to the desk. "I'm afraid you have labored under a misapprehension. I can understand the concern, but there is little in my power to do but abide by the fairness of the lists and the availability of organs. I have at times wished I could step around that, but alas, it is all probably for the best. There is nothing I can do. Do you understand?"

His stare fixed on each of them in turn, and for the quiver of a second Al felt they were being threatened.

Then Corneille relaxed. "Now, if you will excuse me, I have a pressing obligation. Oh, let's be honest. I have a threesome waiting at the country-club lounge, and I'm afraid if I give them too much time in the club bar to enjoy themselves, we'll have a rather useless day of it. *Capisce?*"

Al rose. When the doctor didn't extend a hand, Al didn't wait for one. He turned and led the way out of the office, having never said a single word to Corneille. He suspected Fergie had rather enjoyed her role as woman-in-charge in a relationship, but it hadn't gotten them anywhere, anywhere at all. In fact, they might have just taken a step back.

Al waited until they were outside the building and crossing the pavement to the brick paths of the parking lot before he spoke. "You might have overplayed your cards a little bit back there."

"No matter," she said. "That is one cool cookie. I don't know how anyone would go about getting any favoritism from him, but it wouldn't be the way we went about it. Maybe Doug is right, that the guy is clean as a whistle."

Inside the truck, they both took sips from their containers of lukewarm coffee while waiting for the air conditioning to cool the cab to the level of a tropical rainforest.

"Where are you going to drive Miss Daisy now?" she asked.

"Oh, I've got ideas," he said.

He put the truck in gear and pulled out onto the street. When he saw it was clear around them, he slid out his cell phone, punched in a number, and turned on the speaker so Fergie could hear.

"Clive? Yeah, Al here. Are you finding anything out about those bodies from the landfill?"

"Well, other than what the rats and other critters made a mess of, I found enough to know there wasn't a major organ left among them. Eyes gone too. Helluva pattern. If I had any other assistant than Teddy, they might've gone running out of the room, but she was calm and steady as she would be at a sewing class."

"Where's that lead the other detectives?"

"Nowhere so far. And Clayton says that the Uriah fellow you caught at the scene won't talk. Won't say a single word."

"What puts a man in extreme fear like that?" Al asked.

"A boss with a whip?"

"Exactly."

"I was kidding."

"I wasn't." Al clicked his phone shut.

Al pulled up across the road from the building they sought and left the truck running for the air conditioning. Black letters on a white sign stated Koenig Lab. He couldn't see any cars or other vehicles parked around at the side of the building.

"Sign looks new," Fergie said.

"Yep. Probably since Corneille moved to Austin. You'll recall too that Doug told us the paperwork said LEBC Biologicals, but Nurse Manners said this place."

"Got another call to make. He'll be at work doing his techie thing." Al punched in another number. "Yeah, Meat, it's Al here. I've got a two-cheesecake question maybe you could answer."

"I don't do girls' phone numbers."

Al regretted for a moment having put Meat on speakerphone.

"It's a business. Can you find out who owns it? Get anything you can. Dig as deep as you like. The place is the Koenig Lab out here by the airport."

"I'm all over it like stink," Meat said and hung up.

"Two things," Fergie said. "One. Do you think you might be enabling poor Meat's dietary vices? Two. Did he really say he's on it like stink?"

"Meat is a complex man, Fergie. His choices in life and sugar-based products are the road less taken but the one he has followed with religious fervor."

"Oh, give it a rest."

They sat in silence for twenty minutes, sipping their coffees, and Al started to wish for a bathroom. His phone rang.

"The owner's name is Ian Cage," Meat said. "There wasn't much of any kind of background on him at all."

"That's hardly a whole cheesecake's worth," Al said. "We saw the guy, old-world-looking suit-and-tie guy. You telling me he just popped out of the ground like some kind of mushroom? Go alpha geek on me here, Meat. See if you can get any more than that."

Al hung up and turned to Fergie. Both her eyebrows were all the way up.

"You wanna make out or something while we wait?" he asked.

"Yeah, right." She lifted her cup and took another sip.

Another seven minutes ticked by, Fergie giving Al a nervous glance now and again in case he'd been serious. Al's phone finally rang.

"Well, Al, you are on fire," Meat said, "and shame on me for not drilling deeper when that guy's history was a blank. I did like you asked and dug deeper, a lot deeper."

"And?"

"Turns out this Ian Cage had a legal name change. His former name was Igor Zimorski, a surgeon from the Ukraine who trained in the USSR. He would have had to go through the system here to be a surgeon, so he runs a lab, sticking close to what he knows, apparently. Does that ring the bell on the second cheesecake?"

"Hell, I may have to buy you a half dozen. You've done very well, Meat." Al hung up.

"I believe I could hear him beaming with pride over the phone," Fergie said.

"It was good stuff, though. I just hope all the cheesecakes I get him don't cause him to explode or anything."

"If he's going to, give me warning so I can slip on a gas mask. Okay?"

"Sure. That's all we need, Travis County covered in a fine layer of Meat Jenkins."

"Gosh, you make me glad I haven't had any lunch yet."

"Let's go act like interested prospects," Al said. "What do you say?"

"Sure. Why not? We were such Academy Awards material back there at Corneille's office." The wry twist of her mouth summed up their future as actors.

Al put the truck in gear, swung it around, and went through the open front gates, which were not much different than what he'd seen at the landfill. A one-story warehouse-sized brick building housed Koenig Lab.

"Al, are you just winging it here, or do you have a clear plan?"

"Hey, we've got a Russian surgeon with a name change. Sweet. My gut says we're nosing in the right direction."

"I wish my gut felt as confident."

"Whatever happened to that female intuition of yours?"

"Oh, it's working just fine," she said. "I'm starting to understand why you aren't working on the clock for Clayton."

"Well, to be fair, I didn't play quite this fast and loose when working the job. But we've jostled something, and I think we need to strike while we can."

A couple of places in the lot were marked Visitor, so he pulled into one of those.

The front door was locked. Al pushed the fake-pearl-in-brass-plate bell beside it. He couldn't hear it ring. No one buzzed the door so he could pull it open. Well, he hadn't expected much. Chances were that Ian Cage wouldn't have bought the notion of them as buyers even if Al had had time to have business cards printed up.

Al got out his lockpick kit in its leather folder and bent over. In just over a minute, he tumbled the lock and swung the door open. "I used to be faster."

"You still are at some things."

"Hey!"

"Just pulling your chain. You're fine. You're wonderful. You've ruined me for other men."

"Oh, what a load of... bilge."

He took out his gun, and she hers. He held the door open for her, and they stepped inside to a bare-minimum reception room with the smell of stale dust in the air. He looked around—nothing, and a fine layer of dust covered most of what he saw.

"This isn't the place," he said.

"Doesn't look like it."

They went room to room, finding empty space and more nothing.

"Well, hell." Al got out his cell phone. "Back to the cheesecake factory."

"You're going to give that poor man diabetes, Al."

"I think it's how he wants to go. Probably already has the headstone made."

Meat picked up the receiver. "Wow. This must be my lucky day."

"It will be, Meat, if you can find any other property this Koenig Lab owns. This building is as stale as the original Twinkie."

"I think I ate that Twinkie," Meat said. "Just a minute."

Al heard keys tapping and imagined those sausage-like fingers flying across the keyboard.

"Yeah, Al. Old storage building on a warehouse row not used as much as it used to be. Kinda run down. You sure about this?"

"Just give me the address."

Meat did—the place wasn't far away, a couple of miles closer to town but still in the path of the planes taking off and landing. "You sure you want to go there? Place doesn't sound like much."

"That's just the sort of place I'm looking for," Al said.

When he and Fergie pulled out onto the road, he glanced in the mirror. "Uh-oh."

"What is it?" Fergie turned to look behind them. "Someone's on our tail? I don't see anything."

"You're not supposed to. If it is someone, they're good. Let's hope I'm better."

He drove up the road and timed himself. Just as a large tandem industrial dump truck carrying what looked like thirteen tons of crushed limestone headed their way, Al turned sharp left, cutting right in front of it, and shot down a small side street. The squeal of truck brakes and tires sounded behind them. With the sound still in the air, he cut right, went down a couple blocks of what looked like small one – and two-bedroom homes, little better than shacks–cottages, if he felt generous. Then he took another hard right, eased up to the access road, peeped out, waited, and shot across to an underpass. He pulled up snugly against the inside right wall of the overpass, stopped the truck, and opened the window to listen.

"What are you waiting on?"

His head stayed cocked. "We'll know in a minute."

Five minutes later, he hadn't heard or seen anyone still on their tail, so he put the truck in gear, and they took off again.

CHAPTER TWENTY

A L TURNED HIS TRUCK IN to open front gates, again not much different than he'd seen at the landfill. Old warehouses stood in a row. Scrap yards and wrecking yards spread to the right, filled with many broken cars, from tired to wrecked and piled into gigantic mounds. Down at the far end ahead stood an old stone two-story building that looked as though it might have been a post office or a Masonic lodge back in its day. The building looked as abandoned as the rusting fields of cars except for a new black Lexus parked beside its side door.

"This," Al said, "is the place." It sure didn't look open for business, though.

He saw no parking slots nicely marked Visitor, so he pulled up in the empty lot twenty feet from the front door.

"I take it we're not going to have to be prospective customers looking for a liver now, right?" Fergie asked in a low voice as she got out.

Al shook his head. They eased to the front of the building. Old stone columns stood on either side of the front door, a sturdy wooden slab that looked quite thick. He tried the door, confirming it was locked. He looked but didn't find any bell to ring. Well, he hadn't expected much.

He whispered, "The looks of this place changed my mind. Chances are someone like Ian Cage wouldn't have bought the notion of us as buyers even if I'd had the time to have business cards printed up. And why would he? I doubt he ever deals with the public himself."

He held up a finger and started around the side of the building. The Lexus's trunk gaped open. Al peeked in— mostly boxes of surgical instruments. They would be the hardest to replace. He tried the side door of the building and found it was unlocked. He eased his Sig Sauer out from the small of his back, and Fergie got out her S & W. A cluttered concrete stairway led down a few steps at the side of the crumbling, older-style building. Fergie reached out and touched Al's arm. He leaned closer.

"Are you sure?" she whispered.

He nodded, though he was not stone-cold sure. They'd both agreed that all they had at that point were reasonably good suspicions. Al was aware he had no warrant. He wasn't a cop, just a citizen nosing around. But if he called it in and Clayton deemed it worthy of a warrant, they'd be too late, and the bird would have flown. He started down the stairs.

When they got to the bottom, the door there was slightly ajar. He nodded to Fergie and opened the door. They slipped inside, and at once, he felt glad to be wearing a suit coat. *Man, it feels cold inside, almost open-freezer-door cold.*

The room was brightly lit by fluorescent panels of lights hanging across the ceiling, all on. A shining steel table on the far end of the room stood beside a pair of deep porcelain sinks. A small office had been partitioned off not far from the steel table. Its door stood open. Al heard a voice coming from it. He and Fergie moved that way, checking the steel table with built-in drains. If that table could've talked, it might have told a few grisly tales.

They slipped inside the open door. A man in a white coat put down his phone as Al and Fergie entered. They spread out to either side of the room. He turned and faced them, the same man they'd seen coming out of Dr. Corneille's office. He had slipped a stained white coat on over his suit. His forehead and nose glistened with a light patina of sweat in spite of the frosty cool of the air conditioning.

"What on earth do you people want? We're not open. Can't you see that?" The man's accent had traces of his Russian past, but his English was otherwise good and well practiced.

Al looked around the room. Much of what had been on the walls and in the drawers had been put into boxes that sat on the metal desk. Two straight-backed metal chairs had been placed on the near side. A more comfortable, though worn, rolling chair sat behind the desk.

"Are you planning to move?" Al asked. "Kind of sudden, isn't it?"

"You people are trespassing. I'll call the police."

"Fine with me," Al said, "though out here, you'd be better off with the sheriff's department. You're the hell and gone from the city limits."

Cage didn't reach for his phone.

Al said, "I think I see where we stand."

"Not really, you don't." The voice came from behind Al.

Al turned his head. Doug Chandle stood in the doorway, holding a pistol pointed at Al's back. Over his shoulder was the face of Dennis Cranston, the fired former city detective. *Now, doesn't he look like he's just gotten off a horse! Whooee.* He wore a red-and-white cowboy shirt with pearl buttons, jeans, cowboy boots, and a black cowboy hat with the front of the brim bent down so low it was half over his eyes.

Doug moved to one side so Dennis could step forward to point what looked like a Sam Walker Colt at them.

"Put your gun down on the floor, Al," Doug said. "You too, Fergie."

"Well, this is certainly about the stupidest thing you've ever done, Doug." Fergie put her gun down on the floor.

"Teaming up with Dennis, too. What a couple of gumballs." Al shook his head.

"Hey, no reason to make it personal." Dennis looked far too eager to pull his trigger.

Al stared at the end of the barrel of Dennis's gun, a .44 caliber if he guessed right. Even if Dennis only winged Al, that would disable him and probably send him into shock. From that close, the end of the barrel looked as big around as a drum, a cannon, and the barrel didn't waver a bit.

"I said put the gun down, Al." Doug had caught Al's hesitation, and Al figured him for weighing the odds, which weren't good no matter what Al did. Doug stepped in close, quicker than Al thought possible, and bounced the barrel of his pistol off Al's forehead.

Al felt a trickle of blood running down across his face, past his nose and mouth. Doug stepped closer to Fergie to press the end of the barrel of his gun to her forehead. "Don't even think about it, Al. She'd get it first. Wouldn't want to mess up that pretty face of hers. I've heard how lightning fast you can be when riled, kind of an old-geezer phenomenon. So put that thought on ice."

Al let his gun clatter onto the concrete floor.

Dennis kicked the gun away and pushed the two straight-backed metal chairs to the corner of the desk. Doug waved the end of his gun for Al and Fergie to sit.

Al was slower to sit down than Fergie. He was still weighing his chances, which were far from good. Al calculated distances, wondering whether he could roll and take Doug's legs out from under him before Doug got a shot off.

Dennis went out the office's open door.

"You'd better get scrambling, Doc," Doug said.

"Someone help carry." Cage waved toward the boxes.

"You start without us. We'll help once we've tended to these two."

Al chewed over what Doug meant by that, wishing he hadn't put down his gun, however lousy the odds.

Cage glanced their way then went out the door, carrying two boxes he could barely see over.

Dennis came back into the office with a small spool of steel cable and a stout pair of wire cutters.

Al squirmed on his seat. If Doug's gun was at Al's instead of Fergie's head, Al might have taken any kind of chance. He knew Doug probably planned to kill them both, no matter what. Only the tying them to chairs instead of just shooting them gave Al a thin ray of hope. But that ray was so thin it was feeble. Al tightened his muscles, poised to spring off the chair.

"I mean it. Bang. Red hair everywhere," Doug said.

Al took a slow, deep breath and made himself relax, though not fighting, resisting, was the hardest thing he'd done in a long spell.

Dennis wrapped their hands together and to the sides of the chairs first.

"Not so tight. You'll cut off the circulation," Fergie said.

"Boy, if I had a nickel for every time some lame-ass perp said that to me," Dennis chuckled.

"What an idiot I was to think Doug needed me for anything." Fergie sounded ready to bite.

When Dennis did their ankles, he looped the wire around the bottom leg of the desk so it would hold them in place.

"That asshole was just using me to know how much you knew for sure, Al." Fergie tugged at her wrists. "Or to give you a bum steer if you got too close."

"I know that now," Al said. "My gut felt it, and Tanner seemed to sense it straight off. But that wasn't enough... in time."

"The idea that someone like Doug would need or respect a woman." Fergie's voice had reached a near growl.

"You're right about that." Dennis bent close to Fergie's ear and spoke in a low voice. "If you must know, Doug's a bit of a misogynist, really."

Ian Cage came back into the office and picked up another box. "Is good. You help with boxes now, no?"

"Your accent's going to give you away someday, Zimorski," Al said. *Wasted breath.* Even if Al could get Doug or Dennis riled or off balance for half a second, that didn't matter now, trussed up as he was. Still, he was sure that if Dennis had some duct tape handy, he would have used it to tape Al's mouth shut.

The man glared at Al. "You are bad for biz-ness. I hope you rot in hell." Then he added something in Russian.

"We'll get your damn boxes. Just step lively there," Doug said.

"Don't you forget. You work for me, not I you. I am boss here." Cage spun and headed out the door.

"Yeah, whatever," Doug muttered low.

"A little trouble in paradise, Doug?" Al felt his hands throbbing, and keeping his tone calm became hard, though seeing anger ripple across Doug's face was worth it.

Doug started to say something but kept it to himself. Dennis stood and tossed the wire and cutters into one of the boxes. Dennis spat at Al as he stepped back, the spittle missing Al's face but running down his shirtfront, mixing with blood that fell drop by drop from Al's chin.

"I'm surprised at you, Dennis," Fergie said. "Wasn't a partner of yours gunned down by the Russians once?"

Dennis shrugged. "This guy, he's not *with* the Russians. He just happens to *be* Russian."

Doug shook his head, and Al caught an eye roll. He didn't give that partnership long, but that mattered little to Al and Fergie.

Doug and Dennis each grabbed a couple of boxes, the last of those sitting on Cage's desk.

Al's hands were going numb. He sat in silence as long as he could then finally spoke.

"I'm glad they didn't gag us," Al said.

"Yeah, 'cause I get the feeling I'm going to want to scream," she said.

"Why's that?"

"Take a smell."

Al caught a whiff. *Gas.* When the arson crew arrived later, they could trace the origin of the fire and say accelerants. Then they'd deal with the two charred bodies, Al and Fergie. He could smell the first of the flames. A flame was always hot when started with gas. He knew it for sure: they weren't going to make it out.

He twisted to see if he could look at Fergie. He couldn't quite see her face but could see her mouth pressed tight and tears running down the cheek he could see. The room was getting hotter. *Where's that cool of a few moments ago?*

"Hey, Fergie?"

"Yeah."

"There's something I want—"

"Don't say it, Al."

"What?"

"I mean it. Nothing you might regret."

"But—"

"Not a word."

Al thought he detected a burr of suppressed emotion in her voice despite her attempt to remain firm.

Black smoke rolled into the room. Fergie started to cough, even though Al could tell she was trying not to do so.

His hand could barely reach hers, and their little fingers interlocked. He started reviewing the bucket list in his head. Sure would have liked to go fishing one more time.

Al heard a crash, the slap of leather on stone steps, then a cough that wasn't Fergie's. Steps hurried their way.

"Crap, it's a mess out there." Cam came staggering into the room, waving her hands in front of her face to clear the smoke away. Her short, dirty-blond hair was already moist with sweat, sticking to her forehead in places. Her tanned cheeks shone. Wearing her street clothes, she knelt down beside them and started to untwist the wire that held them to the desk. She glanced around at the empty desktop as she worked. "Didn't think to leave wire cutters or even a set of pliers behind, did they? The sons o' bitches!"

"Glad you came." Fergie coughed.

"Had to back into the front door to smash the place open. Wasn't easy. It was a tough old door. They locked every fucking door and started the fire on the side where they left."

"Aren't you—" Al started.

"Save it for outside. We're going to have to scramble. Al, I'm undoing your hands first so you can help me with Fergie."

They worked in silence except for coughs and muttered curses. As soon as he was free, Al turned to help with Fergie.

Al's fingers could barely work after being tied too tightly for so long, but Cam's fingers were bleeding too as she worked frantically at the wires.

Finally, both Al and Fergie were free. Al and Cam each grabbed one of Fergie's arms, and they started up a set of stone stairs toward the front door, having to skirt an approaching wall of flames and duck low beneath billowing black clouds of nasty-smelling smoke. Then they burst outside, gulping deep breaths. All three of them kept their legs moving, heading toward the crumpled back end of Cam's car, where she'd parked it at a hasty angle near Al's truck. It was a rental, not her 1997 Olds Cutlass, which was why Al hadn't identified the tail earlier. He hoped she'd gotten the insurance package when she'd rented it.

"Those bastards got away," Fergie said as soon as she could speak again.

"I don't know about that," Cam said. "Unlike you, I at least thought to call for backup before coming in."

"You're still active with the department? I thought you were half a step from being in training to be a special agent," Al said.

"Yep, still a deputy." Cam grinned. "Sheriff Clayton and I had a longish sit-down chat, and the long and short of it was that he gave me a chance to redeem myself by following you around like a second skin. Wasn't always easy."

"That must've been some talk Clayton and you had." Al cleared his rasping throat.

"I was at a career crossroads. It led me to make mistakes. He convinced me that someone who learned from mistakes could be as valuable as someone who never made them. He hinted that he'd had to deal with loose cannons before." She looked right at Al. "Clayton told me, 'It's not a good ol' boys network. It's a get-things-done network. But get things done right.' He told me even his best cops sometimes slip off the procedural rails, and he cited your recent flying around without a warrant. Same goes for Special Agent Danielle Cassidy, who he told me is about to get spoken to about the same thing. But Clayton's all about second chances. So here I am. I guess I did resent you some, might have rubbed you the wrong way a time or two."

"I was teetering between punching you or shooting you."

"I probably had it coming. You should see the expressions on your face sometimes, Al. You could make water boil. Speaking of which, I've got some bottles of water in the trunk. Let me get us each one. I feel like I've gargled with lava."

"Thanks," Fergie managed. When Cam moved away, Fergie turned to Al. "Well, you sure have one pip of a friend running the sheriff's department, Al."

"I look forward with relish to having a chat with the man."

Cam came back and gave them each a water bottle.

Al had seen her shove her cell phone back into her pocket. "Has he caught them yet?"

"They're still in pursuit."

"Holy crap." Al dropped his water bottle and ran to his truck. "C'mon."

Fergie had the passenger door open, and Cam clambered into the backseat.

"What the hell, Al?" Fergie asked, but she had the sense to get in and close the door while asking.

Al peeled out. The truck spun in the gravel until he was facing out, and he headed toward the open gate.

"Doug will know about the airport area being a no-fly zone for helicopters. I'm betting he's doubled back in a

THROW THE TEXAS DOG A BONE

loop on them and is heading this way. At least, I would if I was him."

At the road, Al could see the black tire marks of at least one vehicle that had turned hard left. He went that way too, picking up speed.

He'd barely gone a mile when he could see the flicker of red and blue lights. Not far ahead of them he could make out two dark cars coming their way. A hundred yards away, he eased his truck left until he was headed toward them, directly in their lane.

"What the hell are you doing?" Cam yelled from the backseat.

"You might want to buckle up back there."

Al stomped on the brake and spun the truck hard right until the truck had its side to the oncoming cars. At least his side would take it if the cars hit, not Fergie's.

He looked left. The oncoming car was close enough he could see Doug behind the steering wheel with eyes that had popped open wide, about the size of saucers. Doug's shoulders heaved back as he stomped on the brake. Doug's car veered right, shot over into a ditch, bounced, started up the other side toward a phone pole, snapped its guy wire, and came to rest against the wooden post.

When the black Lexus behind Doug went to veer left around Al, Al hit the gas and clipped the back end of the car, putting it into a spin that slid it backward into the ditch on the other side. Its front hood popped open, and steam billowed out.

A column of three sheriff's department cruisers that had been on Doug's tail came to a stop, lights going.

"I believe that looks like Clayton there at the head of the caravan." Al shifted the truck into park and turned off the engine. Cam had the backseat door open and shot out of Al's truck, gun held high in one hand. She ran toward Doug's car.

The deputies in the second and third cruisers rushed toward the crashed cars. As Al got out of the truck, he saw a man running from Doug's car. He heard one shot then another. Clayton was out of his vehicle and lumbering toward where Al had heard the shots.

Al couldn't remember when he'd been as happy to see Clayton or as upset.

———◆———

Clayton saw Cam in a shooting stance with her pistol pointed down at Doug, who lay on his back, looking up at her. Dennis was crumpled a few feet away, screaming. "She fucking shot me. This crazy bitch shot me."

"That was just a warning shot," Cam said. "Doug here can have one too if he does what he's thinking about."

The other deputies rushed up to them, rolled Doug over, got the cuffs on him, and were lifting him to his feet as Clayton got all the way up to them. Cam put her pistol back in its holster.

"I already called for an ambulance, Dennis," Clayton said. "So pipe down. Not another word out of you."

"But—"

"Not a word."

Clayton turned to Doug. "What a disappointment you are to me, son, and just about everyone. It must've been one helluva pile of money they waved at you. Couldn't you see that the stink of something this ripe was going to stick to you once it got busted into the open?"

"I want a lawyer."

"Oh, you'll get one. Read him his rights, in case he's forgotten them. Then get him the hell out of my sight."

"Please," Dennis whimpered.

"Not another word," Clayton said. "Someone get a tourniquet on that leg so he don't bleed out before I get to have a long talk with him." He looked down at Dennis and said, "And, son, I'm gonna expect you to sing as loud and as pretty as Cher after she left Sonny. You hear? A deal's about the only hope you have at this point."

———◆———

Ten minutes later, Al watched Clayton come back to where he and Fergie sat waiting on the lowered tailgate of Al's truck. Al had heard the shots and seen a cluster of deputies gather close.

"Caught 'em just down the road. Easy peasy," Clayton said as he got within earshot. He lifted the front of his hat's brim up an inch. "Well, not entirely easy. Doug and Dennis kicked up a fuss, and Dennis caught a slug in the kneecap. You oughta hear that fellow cuss. Would have turned my Aunt Blanche's hair gray in a heartbeat."

"Let me guess," Al said. "Cam was the one who popped him in the knee."

"Yep. Who saw that coming? She still has a few rough edges. Give it time." Clayton glanced down the road, in the direction of the buildings. Black smoke billowed out in the direction the wind was blowing. In the distance, from the other way, came the approaching sirens of several fire trucks. "Got Zimorski too."

"You know his real name?" Al looked up at Clayton, his neck feeling like tired rubber. He could probably crawl under the truck and take a nap right there.

"Meat Jenkins let me know."

"He was in on this?"

"Meat *does* work for the department, after all. You did some fine, relentless digging, Al. We were already on the way here when we heard from Cam, who was on your tail.

225

She'd have been to you sooner, but you're too good for her to tail close. You ditched her altogether. Lucky for us, Meat had a hunch where you were headed."

Al's truck was dented—probably his fault. His wrists and ankles were raw with wire marks, but so were Fergie's, and he looked down at a suit that was going to need some help if he was ever to be buried in it. He was sure there was a half-full-glass side to everything, but he was going to need a few moments to get there.

"Put in a chit for any expenses or repairs." Clayton glanced toward Al's truck.

"Does any of this have to do with an overzealous FBI agent trying to make a name for herself instead of just doing her job and cooperating with locals?"

Clayton's large head turned back to Al. "Now, you know I would never do anything to interfere with a federal agency."

But you would damned well resent it.

"The thing is," Clayton said, "every organization gets its occasional maverick who forgets or bends the rules of good procedure. Might be a guy rushing into a place without a warrant or going ballistic on a fellow who'd just killed his partner. You wouldn't know anyone like that, would you?"

Al's mouth opened then closed. He had nothing to add.

Cam came walking toward them, getting there just in time to hear that. She shared a tired grin.

"Well, all I know," Clayton said, "is I've got a Russian doctor who is one of several folks here due for a real up-close-and-personal chat with me. We'll take Cam back to her rental, see if the fire hasn't destroyed everything. We're lucky the fool packed all that hard evidence in his trunk. I'd like to suggest that you and Fergie go home and take a rest. I do believe you're looking in worse shape than your dog, Al. Though I have one more little chore you might like to be in on if you're up to it."

Al felt a tightness on his forehead, from the bandages one of the deputies had applied from a first-aid kit. He was tired to the toes of his boots but glanced toward Fergie then nodded. "Sure. Why not?"

Clayton grinned and spun on his boot heel, and they followed him toward his waiting cruiser.

———◆———

In the line of people waiting to pass through security, Dr. August Corneille reached up to run fingers through his hair at one temple, self-conscious about having dyed it black. He'd never used a package of hair dye before and had made a horrible mess, and then, just as he got into line, he'd remembered he wouldn't look exactly like the picture on his passport. The passport was under a different name, but he'd forgotten the photo matched the way he had looked. He rehearsed natural-sounding explanations, figuring he could throw in the idea of trying to please a lady as the reason. He hoped he wouldn't need to explain at all, that they would just wave him on through.

The PA system boomed out another message about leaving bags unattended. It seemed to him the people in line around him, clutching their IDs and boarding passes, crowded closer to him than necessary, and the line moved forward at a pace that would put a snail to sleep. *He should have chartered a plane. Damn the parsimony or twisted logic that had let him argue that riding coach would be less conspicuous.*

He heard the hum of something new in the relentless airport noise, above the chattering of people among themselves or on cell phones, all of it accompanied by that blasted PA system, now speaking in Spanish. Men were pushing through the lines from either side. He didn't care for people, especially that close. *Too late now to rethink his choice.* He could make out uniforms pushing through the crowd, coming his way.

Those around him rose on their toes and peered with interest at what was going on. He mimed them to fit in. He'd let his usual erect posture slump and had let his chin and cheeks go to stubble. *Damn it, he was doing all he could.*

The crowd parted. Corneille first recognized the guy Doug had told him was Al Quinn, the fellow who'd come to his office with a particularly lame story, which had sent a chill up his spine all the same. The tall redhead stood next to him. They looked haggard, and Quinn had a white bandage on his forehead. However, they looked chipper compared to the way Corneille felt. His smug confidence had gone out the window. *It had become a fox hunt, he was the fox, and the hunt was almost over.*

He recognized the man next to Quinn, too. Corneille had seen him on television enough during the past election. That would be Sheriff Clayton. He was grinning, the same grin he'd shared on the night he'd won the last election to retain his job as sheriff.

Quinn pointed, and the sky marshals and airport security came in a wave toward Corneille, who lowered his carry-on bag and raised his hands. He had that sinking feeling that it was going to take more than being a little glib to talk himself out of this one.

CHAPTER TWENTY-ONE

A L'S EYES FLUTTERED OPEN.

"Hey, come out here!" Maury yelled again. His shout carried in from the other side of the closed bedroom door.

Under the covers, Fergie's naked back pressed up against him in a classic spoon. He lifted an arm and checked his watch—just a bit after eight. Despite having been exhausted when coming home, showering, and collapsing into bed, he felt her soft skin, smelled the nape of her neck, and felt himself stirring.

The door swung open, and Tanner jumped up and barked. Maury and Bonnie came rushing to the bedside.

"I mean it," Maury said. "Come now and see what's on the news."

"We don't even have a television," Al said.

"We do now," Bonnie said. "The doorbell rang early this morning, real early, and some boxes were on the porch. You have a new television and a new stereo too."

Fergie turned onto her back and pulled the covers up to her chin.

"Who are they from?" Al lay on his back as well.

"No card on them, but it was a sheriff's-department patrol car I saw pulling away," Bonnie said. "Maury's been busy setting them up. I'm guessing there's something your buddy the sheriff didn't want us to miss."

"That Clayton is one piece of work." Maury stared down

at the covers, maybe trying to make out some of Fergie's form beneath them.

"Small price, I think, for darn near getting us both killed." Fergie gave a small cough.

Al figured it would take a day or two before everything cleared out of their lungs.

"I mean it. Hurry out here." Maury spun and rushed out of the room, and Tanner ran after him.

"Get dressed first if you like," Bonnie said. "But hurry. This is good. You might even want to put off the quickie you're thinking about, Al."

"Me?"

"You can lie all you want, but the pup tent in the covers tells only the truth." She giggled, spun, and headed out of the bedroom, closing the door behind her.

Minutes later, Al and Fergie came out into the living room and accepted the warm mugs of coffee Bonnie held out to them. They settled onto the couch and looked at a screen twice as big as the one Al had previously owned.

The coverage was already underway, some of it looping over and over as an announcer spoke. The footage showed a familiar-enough scene: guys wearing black tactical gear smashing into a building from all sides. The camera flicked to another scene. The difference there was that the SWAT guys didn't have FBI on their backs. They were city police. The next clip showcased the county's tactical team sweeping in on another building.

"Well, the boys and girls were sure having fun last night," Al said to Fergie.

"Aw, you just wish you could have been there. What a party!" She winked at him.

Tanner climbed up onto the couch and wriggled in between Fergie and Al. He stared at the television too. Al put a hand on his back, and Fergie put her hand on his.

The women pouring out of the buildings represented a wide range, too. Al saw Hispanic, Asian, and even some that might've been Russian. Law enforcement was having quite a night of it, raiding places Al hadn't been aware existed.

"I'm guessing Ian Cage, or Zimorski if you rather, sang like a scalded canary," Al said. "He had to be looking death row in the face with all they had on him for killing all those women here in Texas."

"These poor women here." Fergie pointed to the screen, where they were being herded out of the building where'd they been indentured to ply the oldest profession.

"Poor women? I don't think so." Bonnie sat on the floor in front of the new television, her feet curled under her, like a kid on Christmas morning. "You know what those are? They're free women now. They've been rescued."

Maury nodded.

"You know, Al," Bonnie said, "I'm just starting to figure out what it is you do."

"Really? How so?"

"You're a rescuer. You rescued Tanner. You rescued Maury from a life of doing whatever it is I'm still trying to wean him of."

"Hey," Maury said.

"And you rescued me from that job at the hospital." Bonnie beamed up at him.

Al started to say something.

Bonnie beat him to it. "I know. You can't pay me nurse's wages forever to take care of Maury, though you gotta admit that the health care has extended to a whole new personal level. But doesn't he glow like a new penny now?" She gave Maury a wink and turned back to the big screen. She waved a hand toward the women huddling in groups in front of the television cameras. "And you saved them.

You sure enough did. The others can take the credit, but you're the one who really did something about it."

"What did Al save me from?" Fergie said.

"I don't know. I guess we can rule out virginity. How about your status as an amateur?"

Fergie threw a pillow at Bonnie that bounced off her shoulder. Tanner barked at the bit of excitement.

"You're right about one thing," Fergie said. "Al was in it for the right reasons. That Cassidy woman was on a campaign, but like Clayton said, her agenda was to boost herself. All the human-trafficking stuff was just a sexy arena for her to have her successes. But it started to wear and show through. They were just a step for her, a step up."

"And we all see where that got her," Al said.

"Yep. She missed out altogether when the big roundup happened," Fergie said. "Ah, here comes the real dog-and-pony show."

She was right—the press conference. Clayton stood there on the podium with the chief of the city police, as well as Alex Manchester, the agent in residence at Austin's FBI office. However, he saw no sign of Danielle Cassidy. Al relaxed and felt Fergie do the same.

The announcer, a normally calm local anchor who seemed unusually stoked for once, was calling this raid the biggest in city and county history and went on to say how it had been a coordinated effort among the various city, county, and federal groups of law enforcement. The camera panned across the faces of the seated leaders who would soon speak. To Clayton's credit, he didn't break out into a grin, but Al could tell he was dying to share a really big one.

"Are you sure this is where you want to have your celebration lunch?" Fergie asked.

"You mean our celebrating being alive?" Al parked the truck away from the construction going on next door to the Flying Dragon restaurant, though the site was no longer active. Still, that side of the parking lot had a few scattered boards and cinder blocks he'd as soon avoid.

"Ah, my number-one customer." Gyp came rushing toward them the moment he spotted them coming in the door.

Al didn't get time to explain to Fergie that he and Gyp had in the past discussed the Charlie Chan novels. The "number-one son" business had especially tickled Gyp.

"I fix you very special meal. You recall time you like squid with black mushroom in garlic sauce. I fix for you. For lady, I make jellyfish salad. Rare treat not on menu." He put a pot of tea on the table and rushed off.

"Gee. Jellyfish," Fergie said. "It seems all is forgiven about that ATF situation."

"If there ever was one," Al said. "The jellyfish salad is not too bad. It's mixed with seaweed. Relax. You can have some of my squid. We'll share."

Gyp came bustling back to their table with a couple of spring rolls and plates.

As he put them in place, Al said, "Hey, it's a shame about your neighbor, Dong-Ho Kwon. I hear he got swept up in that business last night—owned the Red Barn and a couple more places. He was turning into quite a local power."

"Yeah, he get arrested. Too bad. Ha. Ha." Gyp grinned then shot off again.

"Imagine having a restaurant like this, and someone is going to open a Korean one right next to it. That could sure put a damper on things, especially if the owner is a no-good guy, one of those at the heart of this trafficking business."

"You think Gyp played you a little on that one? Or at the least sowed some seeds with Cam?"

"I don't know if 'played' is the right word."

"What if he is embarrassed about accusing you of sending the ATF around?"

"What if they weren't ATF at all but agents nosing around Dong-Ho Kwon, and their need to be around went away when Kwon went down?"

"Yet your pal Gyp thinks you're the one who helped eliminate his competition."

"He's free to think what he likes. If it makes him feel good, I'm okay with that."

"So he sees himself as the master manipulator here?"

"Hard to tell about ol' Gyp. Maybe he is. As I've said, he can be downright inscrutable. He did give me a hard steer toward the Red Barn, and once the shell companies were stripped away, that was all Dong-Ho Kwon."

"Which worked out pretty well for him since the threat of a competing restaurant right next to him went away."

"A lot of good came of it all too, especially for some of those women, who will be saved from what lay ahead."

"It still turns my stomach to think just because some of those women were getting older they were deemed less attractive—sold off like used auto parts."

Al took a sip of his hot tea. "The whole thing comes down to agendas. Sure, Gyp probably had one, something to do with a competitor, this Dong-Ho Kwon. But Cam had one as well, as did Doug and Dennis, along with the good Dr. Corneille and Ian Cage, whatever his real name was. Even my trusted old friend Sheriff Clayton had an agenda. We just happened to wind up in the middle of that maelstrom and are lucky enough to have come out of it alive."

"Lucky indeed." Fergie reached for the teapot. "How do you know I didn't have an agenda as well? And what about yourself?"

"Well, I did get a pretty nice dog out of it."

She punched his shoulder as Gyp Sing headed their way with another tray. "Save room for desert. Lychees. You know how much you like lychees, my good friend Al."

"Okay, let's get this show on the road," Clayton said. He stood looking into an empty room through one-way glass. "By the way, Al, turned out that Dr. Corneille had a ticket to Mexico in his hand. Another lined up to São Paulo after that. Like Ian Cage, he sang louder than a dozen Mormon Tabernacle Choirs. Helping uncover what he was up to made me look pretty good. I owe you."

"Thanks for this," Al said.

"Not a worry." Clayton winked at Fergie, who stood on the other side of Al, with Bonnie and Maury next to her, a real family sort of gathering.

"Well, it's certainly a worry to me. This is highly irregular," Bobbie Briscoe said. He stood on the other side of Clayton, wearing a blue suit and red tie, the same ones he wore in his television spots, Al was pretty sure. If he'd just snap his fingers once and say, "It's as easy as snap," he could've convinced Al he was in a commercial.

"What's to worry about, Briscoe? You've seen a hundred of these lineups. It's all on the up-and-up."

"But it was established earlier that no one at the burgled house was a direct witness of the subjects." Bobbie reached to straighten his tie in a move that reminded Al of Rodney Dangerfield's "I get no respect" bit.

"Not entirely true," Clayton said. "No person may have seen them. But there was a witness."

"What the hell are you talking about?"

"Wait and learn, Briscoe. You'll notice that your two guys are mixed in with a full lineup, at least two more than we usually use. You have no squawk. None whatsoever."

Men were led in and lined up in front of a wall that measured their heights. They turned to face the wall where Al, Clayton, Bobbie, and the others all looked through the one-way glass. Toby Buchanan smiled, though with fewer green teeth than before. He probably shouldn't have. He was confident. They were practically home free.

A door opened from the other side, and a deputy, skinny Pudge Simmons, came out beside Teddy, who was leading Tanner on a leash. Teddy wasn't a necessary touch, but she'd pleaded for one more chance to be with the dog. Clayton had relented since she rarely ever asked for anything. As soon as Tanner was in the room, he tugged at his leash, started barking, and pulled Teddy along until they stood right in front of Toby.

Toby leaned out and looked down the row at Donnie, giving him a "keep your mouth shut" look.

But Donnie wasn't having any of it. He yelled, "Everybody knows you did it, that you're the one who kicked the dog. I saw you. They're not dumping hurting a cop's dog on me."

"Hey, make him shut up." Bobbie Briscoe tried to push his way around Clayton and get to the door.

"Shut the hell up, Donnie. Just keep your trap closed," Briscoe yelled. He wasn't able to get past Clayton.

"I think it's a little late for that, Briscoe. Everything's recorded. You know that. And isn't part of your pitch that if you don't win a case for your clients, they owe you nothing? With this and what we got from the pawnshop, I think we have your boys cold. It sounds like Donnie is ready to cut a deal. You can sit in on that, of course. Looks like you may end up defending these two for free."

Briscoe still struggled to get around the sheriff.

Clayton leaned around Bobbie to wink at Al and the rest of Al's household. "The witness has spoken."

OTHER BOOKS BY RUSS HALL

Thrillers

To Hell and Gone in Texas (An Al Quinn Novel)

A Turtle Roars in Texas (An Al Quinn Novel)

Island

Wildcat Did Growl

Talon's Grip

World Gone Wrong

Mysteries

The Blue-Eyed Indian

Bones of the Rain

South Austin Vampire

No Murder Before Its Time

Black Like Blood

Goodbye, She Lied

Westerns

Bent Red Moon

Bullets in the Wind

Three-Legged Horse

Young Adult Sci Fi

Inside Jupiter

ABOUT THE AUTHOR

Russ Hall is author of fifteen published fiction books, most in hardback and subsequently published in mass market paperback by Harlequin's Worldwide Mystery imprint and Leisure Books. He has also co-authored numerous non-fiction books, most recently *Do You Matter: How Great Design Will Make People Love Your Company* (Financial Times Press, 2009) with Richard Brunner, former head of design at Apple and *Now You're Thinking* (Financial Times Press, 2011), and *Identity* (Financial Times Press, 2012) with Stedman Graham, Oprah's companion.

Russ has been a nonfiction editor for major publishing companies, ranging from HarperCollins (then Harper & Row), Simon & Schuster, to Pearson. He has lived in Ohio, Connecticut, Florida, North Carolina, and New York, and he currently calls Texas home. Russ is a long-time member of the Mystery Writers of America, Western Writers of America, and Sisters in Crime. He is a frequent judge for writing organizations.

In 2011, he was awarded the Sage Award, by the

Barbara Burnett Smith Mentoring Authors Foundation—a Texas award for the mentoring author who demonstrates an outstanding spirit of service in mentoring, sharing, and leading others in the mystery writing community. In 1996, he won the Nancy Pickard Mystery Fiction Award for short fiction.

www.ingramcontent.com/pod-product-compliance
Lightning Source LLC
Chambersburg PA
CBHW030255200626
46816CB00002BA/650